CURVEBALL

ALSO BY DEREK JETER

The Contract

Hit & Miss

Change Up

Fair Ball

Baseball Genius

Double Play

CURVEBALL

DEREK JETER

with Paul Mantell

JETER CHILDREN'S

SIMON & SCHUSTER BOOKS FOR YOUNG READERS

New York London Toronto Sydney New Delhi

SIMON & SCHUSTER BOOKS FOR YOUNG READERS
An imprint of Simon & Schuster Children's Publishing Division
1230 Avenue of the Americas, New York, New York 10020
This book is a work of fiction. Any references to historical events, real people,
or real places are used fictitiously. Other names, characters, places, and events
are products of the author's imagination, and any resemblance to actual
events or places or persons, living or dead, is entirely coincidental.
SIMON & SCHUSTER BOOKS FOR YOUNG READERS
is a trademark of Simon & Schuster, Inc.
For information about special discounts for bulk purchases, please contact Simon
& Schuster Special Sales at 1-866-506-1949 or business@simonandschuster.com.
The Simon & Schuster Speakers Bureau can bring authors to your live event. For
more information or to book an event, contact the Simon & Schuster Speakers
Bureau at 1-866-248-3049 or visit our website at www.simonspeakers.com.
Also available in a Simon & Schuster Books for Young Readers hardcover edition
Book design by Krista Vossen
The text for this book was set in Centennial LT Std.
Manufactured in the United States of America
0319 OFF
First Simon & Schuster Books for Young Readers paperback edition April 2019
2 4 6 8 10 9 7 5 3 1
The Library of Congress has cataloged the hardcover edition as follows:
Names: Jeter, Derek, 1974– author. | Mantell, Paul, author.
Title: Curveball / Derek Jeter with Paul Mantell.
Description: First edition. | New York : Simon & Schuster Books for Young Readers,
[2018] | "Jeter Children's." | Summary: While spending the summer with his
extended family in New Jersey, Derek finds a team he can play baseball with and
earns money to take his best friend to a Yankees game.
Identifiers: LCCN 2017035621| ISBN 9781534409897 (hardcover) |
ISBN 9781534409910 (eBook)) | ISBN 9781534409903 (pbk)
Subjects: LCSH: Jeter, Derek, 1974–—Childhood and youth—Juvenile fiction. |
CYAC: Jeter, Derek, 1974–—Childhood and youth—Fiction. | Baseball—Fiction. |
Grandparents—Fiction. | Family life—New Jersey—Fiction. | New York Yankees
(Baseball team)—Fiction. | New Jersey—History—20th century—Fiction. | BISAC:
JUVENILE FICTION / Sports & Recreation / Baseball & Softball. | JUVENILE
FICTION / Social Issues / Friendship. | JUVENILE FICTION / Social Issues / Values
& Virtues. Classification: LCC PZ7.J55319 Cur 2018 | DDC [Fic]—dc23
LC record available at https://lccn.loc.gov/2017035621

*To my grandmother, whose love of
the Yankees became my own and whose
encouragement never wavered*
—D. J.

A Note About the Text

The rules of Little League followed in this book are the rules of the present day. There are six innings in each game. Every player on a Little League baseball team must play at least two innings of every game in the field and have at least one at bat. In any given contest, there is a limit on the number of pitches a pitcher can throw, in accordance with age. Pitchers who are eight years old are allowed a maximum of fifty pitches in a game, pitchers who are nine or ten years old are allowed seventy-five pitches per game, and pitchers who are eleven or twelve years old are allowed eighty-five pitches.

Dear Reader,

Curveball is inspired by some of my experiences growing up. The book portrays the values my parents instilled in me and the lessons they have taught me about how to remain true to myself and embrace the unique differences in everyone around me.

Curveball is based on the lesson that the right role models serve as guides for success. This is one of the principles I have lived by in order to achieve my dreams. I hope you enjoy reading!

Derek Jeter

DEREK JETER'S 10 LIFE LESSONS

1. Set Your Goals High (*The Contract*)

2. Think Before You Act (*Hit & Miss*)

3. Deal with Growing Pains (*Change Up*)

4. The World Isn't Always Fair (*Fair Ball*)

5. **Find the Right Role Models (*Curveball*)**

6. Don't Be Afraid to Fail

7. Have a Strong Supporting Cast

8. Be Serious but Have Fun

9. Be a Leader, Follow the Leader

10. Life Is a Daily Challenge

CONTRACT FOR DEREK JETER

1. Family Comes First. Attend our nightly dinner.
2. Be a Role Model for Sharlee. (She looks to you to model good behavior.)
3. Do Your Schoolwork and Maintain Good Grades (As or Bs).
4. Bedtime. Lights out at nine p.m. on school nights.
5. Do Your Chores. Take out the garbage, clean your room on weekends, and help with the dishes.
6. Respect Others. Be a good friend, classmate, and teammate. Listen to your teachers, coaches, and other adults.
7. Respect Yourself. Take good care of your body and your mind. Avoid alcohol and drugs. Surround yourself with positive friends with strong values.
8. Work Hard. You owe it to yourself and those around you to give your all. Do your best in everything that you do.
9. Think Before You Act.

Failure to comply will result in the loss of playing sports and hanging out with friends. Extra-special rewards include attending a Major League Baseball game, choosing a location for dinner, and selecting another event of your choice.

CONTENTS

CONTENTS

CURVEBALL

Chapter One

SUMMER DREAMS

Crack!

As soon as the bat hit the ball, Derek knew it was coming his way. From his crouch he tracked the screaming liner with his eyes, timing his leap, upward and to his right. At the last instant he stretched his arm as far as he could.

It seemed to Derek in that nanosecond, as he flew through the air, that he really was flying! It also seemed to him that his arm extended farther than the possible limits of human arm-stretching. . . .

And the ball hit his mitt—right at the outer edge of the webbing! Derek squeezed the ball tightly as he fell back to earth, held it as he hit the dirt of the infield and kept skidding.

"*Two! Two! Two!*" someone was shouting at him. Derek knew what that meant. He had a chance to get the runner trying for second base, making two outs in one incredible play—if he could just get up and throw to second on time!

Somehow he got the throw off, and Willie Randolph grabbed it in his mitt. At that exact millisecond the runner slid into Willie's glove. "OUT!" the umpire yelled.

"*Way to go, Derek!*" shouted his best friend Dave from Kalamazoo, who was manning third base.

"*Attaboy, Derek!*" said Ron Guidry, the pitcher, congratulating him as they both stepped into the Yankees dugout. "*Thanks for saving my bacon.*"

"*Great play, kid!*" Don Mattingly said, tipping his captain's cap.

Suddenly Derek found himself outside the stadium, in the parking lot. The game was over, but he was still in uniform. Next to him a car was gunning its engine—a sports car . . . and in the driver's seat, Dave Winfield. Derek's all-time favorite ballplayer!

"*You played a great game today, kid,*" he told Derek as he gunned the engine. "*Awesome job for an eleven-year-old.*"

HUH?

Eleven? What in the—

Derek sat up in bed with a start. *Wow,* he thought as he let his heart calm down in the darkness of the bedroom. *That was some dream.*

Across the room his sister, Sharlee, lay peacefully in

her bed, softly snoring. Derek looked over at the alarm clock. It was just after five in the morning.

Hearing the revving of a car motor, he realized that was what had woken him up. He went to the window. It was still dark outside, but at the far end of the yard, where the property met the road, his grandpa's old pickup truck was just pulling out of the long driveway.

Sharlee and Derek were spending the summer with their grandparents in Greenwood Lake, New Jersey, just as they did every year. And like on every other day while they were there, Grandpa was already on his way to work. Six days a week, and half days on Sundays too. That's what it was like to be the chief caretaker of a church, which was what Derek's grandpa had been for many, many years.

Grandpa always came home from work hungry and tired. Most evenings, all he could do was eat dinner, watch a little TV, and fall asleep—usually before Sharlee's bedtime, let alone Derek's. So it was mostly Grandma who was able to spend time with the kids.

She was the one in charge of the kids all day. She cooked for them, did the wash, cleaned the house, played with them, and tended to their cuts and bruises. The amazing part was, she almost always seemed to *enjoy* it. To Derek she had always been a kind of—well, not superhero, maybe, but superperson. She'd had thirteen kids of her own, including Derek's mom, and she'd raised them all into fine, upstanding grown-ups, and now she was helping watch all the grandkids, too. He hoped that when he was a grown-up, everyone would love and respect him the way everyone in the family did Grandma.

Derek looked out the open window. He could hear the crickets chirping. The sky was starting to get lighter.

He didn't feel the least bit tired. In fact, he felt restless. He couldn't wait for the morning to get going so that the usual fun could start!

He and Sharlee had already been here a few days, but it had rained a ton. They'd hung out a lot with their cousins, who all lived in the area, and some of whom always managed to end up sleeping over at Grandma and Grandpa's. They'd all gone bowling once, and to a movie another time.

But Derek hadn't been swimming in the lake much yet this summer—and that was where most of the fun happened around here.

Right now everyone was still asleep. Derek got dressed quietly, washed up, and went down to the kitchen to make a bowl of cereal, and wait for Grandma to come downstairs.

She was almost always the first awake, in order to make sure everyone's breakfast was ready before they even got downstairs, but she wasn't the first today. Grandpa's truck had seen to that by waking Derek up extra early. Still, Grandma was sure to be down in a few minutes, well before Sharlee, who usually slept till eight o'clock at least.

As he made "pre-breakfast" Derek thought back to the dream that had woken him up so early. What had been so great about it was that he and his friend Dave had been playing for the Yankees—the *real* Yankees, including Mattingly, Randolph, Guidry, and especially Dave Winfield.

Winfield had been a great player for years, and Derek idolized him. Derek knew everything there was to know about Winfield. Not just because he was a great ballplayer, but also because he was a great person. He'd even started his own charity!

Derek knew that, because he had done a report on Winfield last term at school, when they'd had to write about their role models—the people you look up to and listen to because you want to be like them in some way or other.

Derek had considered writing about his mom or dad, or grandma or grandpa. But his teacher had told them all to look for role models outside the immediate family. So Derek had chosen Winfield, naturally.

Derek hoped he could someday be like Winfield— except that he wanted to play shortstop for the Yankees, not right field. Derek felt deep inside that if he worked hard enough, and kept improving his game . . .

That was the thing that had been eating at him ever since he'd arrived for the summer. His game.

Sure, everything was great here in New Jersey, as usual. But Derek had just come off a great season of playing baseball, with his dad as his coach. They'd won the league championship—Derek's first title ever!

He'd been so psyched by the end of the season that he never wanted to stop playing ball. And as much fun as he always had with his grandma and grandpa, there was no summer Little League here that he could be a part of.

Derek feared he'd lose some of his new baseball skills over the summer. In fact, he wouldn't have another chance to get into a real game until Little League started up again next spring, almost a whole year from now.

Well, at least when Dave comes, Derek thought, *we'll be able to work on our game a little.* Dave was a good player, even though he'd been playing baseball for only a couple of years. Golf was Dave's real passion, and someday he hoped to go professional in that sport. For him baseball was just a way to have fun. But he had enough athletic talent that he could go far in baseball, too.

Derek knew why he'd seen Dave in the dream about the Yankees. Dave was going to be coming to visit him here in New Jersey in three weeks. Derek was psyched just thinking about it. He'd show Dave the lake, and the Castle, and introduce him to everybody, and get him involved in all the family fun.

The two of them would also find time, he hoped, to play some mini-golf, or pitch and putt—maybe even go to a driving range. Derek was sure he could persuade Grandma to take them.

Best of all, Derek was looking forward to taking Dave to his first major-league baseball game—at Yankee Stadium! Derek's grandmother always organized a family outing to a Yankees game every summer, always in early August, which was when Dave was due to be here.

The whole family came along, including Grandma, aunts, uncles, and cousins—even the little kids. It was always a blast. They practically took up a whole section in the upper deck in right field. Derek couldn't wait to share it all with his best friend in the world.

Or rather, with *one* of his *two* best friends. The other was Vijay Patel, but Vijay was in India for the whole summer with his family. They were there to attend a family wedding. Vijay hadn't been able to join Derek in New Jersey, but hey, there was always next year, right?

Grandma came into the kitchen just as Derek was finishing his cereal. "Well! Look who's the early bird!" she said with a chuckle. "Since when did you turn into an early riser?"

"I heard Grandpa's truck pulling out of the driveway."

Grandma frowned. "If I've told your grandpa once, I've told him a dozen times, to get that muffler fixed." She glanced at Derek's empty cereal bowl. "Aha! I see you've already made yourself breakfast. I guess you won't be wanting any of my homemade pancakes, then—"

"Yes! Yes, I want some!" Derek shouted, then put a hand

over his mouth. He hadn't meant to yell so loudly when everyone else was still asleep. Besides him and Sharlee, there were always other cousins staying at the house.

"Hmm," said Grandma. "I suppose I could let you have two breakfasts, just for today," she joked. "After all, you're a growing boy." She turned toward the pantry, going for the flour.

"Grandma, never mind. I can wait," Derek said suddenly, hopping out of his chair. "I want you to see how far I can hit the ball now! Come on out into the yard, and I'll show you!"

"It'll have to be a short session," she warned. "Aunt Dorien is coming at seven thirty to drop off Jessie and Alfie on her way to work, and I've got those pancakes to mix up for everyone."

Aunt Dorien worked in New York City, about an hour away by car. She was a manager at a hospital. Her kids, Jessica and little Alfie, were five and three years old. Grandma would be making pancakes for them, too, and then they'd all head over to the Castle for a day at the lake with the rest of the family.

Grandma Dorothy had lots of responsibilities, but her main one was watching all the family's kids all day while they played down at the lake, which was about a five-minute drive away.

The property belonging to Derek's extended family featured a huge old stone house, known as "the Castle" because it really did look like one. It had been built by some rich guy long ago but had since been made into several apartments, most of which were lived in by Derek's relatives.

There were other, smaller homes on the property too, as well as a large lawn leading down to the lake. Derek's cousins played all kinds of games on the lawn—volleyball, tag, touch football, soccer, and of course Wiffle ball, which always frustrated Derek.

He had cousins who were his age or older. But there were also lots of little kids running all over the place, so it wasn't safe to hit a baseball, or even a softball. And after years of playing hardball in Little League, Wiffle ball just didn't do it for Derek anymore.

There was a public beach in the town of Greenwood Lake, but the family members almost never went there. Why would they, when all they had to do was jump into the lake off the cement boat dock at the Castle? There was a wooden floating platform about a hundred feet out, where they could rest if they were tired, and pretend they were on a boat or a ship.

Yes, there was always someone to have fun with, just not this early in the morning.

"I should be making breakfast for the others," Grandma objected. "Sharlee and the rest will be up in a little while, if they aren't already."

"Don't worry. They'll yell when they want food. Here,

put this on," he said, giving her his mitt. "I'll hit 'em to you.

"I saw you hit some whoppers," said Grandma. "Down by the lake, when you were playing Wiffle ball the other day. You were really whacking that ball!"

"Wiffle ball?" Derek moaned. "Wiffle balls don't go far when you hit them. You've got to see me hit a real baseball!"

"And who's going to chase down all these home runs of yours?" she asked. But he was already jogging over to the far end of the yard, by the woods at the edge of the property. Grandma followed him. Raising his bat as she tossed the ball, he swung with all his might.

The ball dropped harmlessly to the ground behind him. He'd been in such a rush to show off for her that he hadn't remembered to keep his eye on the ball. "Wait, wait!" he said.

"I didn't see anything," she called. "Did you hit anything yet?"

He could see the grin on her face. Grandma loved to tease him. She loved all her grandkids and would have dropped everything to spend time with any of them. She'd been Derek's biggest fan ever since he could remember. Why, it was all because of her that he'd become a Yankees fan.

His second swing was right on the money. The bat hit the ball with a sharp *CRACK!* It sailed way past Grandma and right out onto the road. "Whoa!" she cried as she jogged carefully across to fetch it. "Who was that? Mickey Mantle? Joe DiMaggio?"

Derek laughed. On his next swing he hit one way over her head. It landed on the road and took a high bounce onto the neighbor's lawn across the street.

After she'd retrieved it, Grandma walked the ball back in. "Derek, we'd better have you hit it the other way, before you wind up denting somebody's car."

So they switched sides. That might have helped avoid an accident, but it didn't help Grandma any. Time after time she had to make her way into the woods to find the balls he'd hit past her.

"This yard isn't big enough for you anymore," she told him after six or seven swings, when she'd had enough of picking her way through fallen branches and underbrush. "We've got to find you another place to hit. Otherwise we're going to run out of baseballs mighty fast!"

"I told you I got better at hitting!" Derek said proudly. "I can field better too!"

"I'll bet you can." She put an arm around him. "But not before you have some pancakes in you." She kissed him on the forehead, and they went back into the house.

There was still no sign of Sharlee or the others, but once they smelled the pancakes, they'd be down in a hurry, Derek knew.

"You really have come a long way in one short year," Grandma told him as she mixed the batter. "I guess Wiffle ball doesn't quite do it for you anymore, like in the old days when you were little."

She poured the batter into the frying pan, and it sizzled, making a delicious smell. "Maybe when your friend Dave is here, you can get into a game or two over at the high school field. Logan and Andrew play softball over there sometimes."

Logan and Andrew were cousins of his who were in high school. Derek had already thought of asking them about it, but he wasn't really into softball either. For him it had always been hardball or nothing.

But her mention of Dave had reminded him of something else—he needed to ask her about Dave coming with them to Yankee Stadium on his visit. He was sure she'd say yes, but he'd already promised Dave, and he didn't want to leave it till the last minute to get permission from Grandma.

"Oh, by the way," she said, before he got a chance to open his mouth. "I forgot to tell you. I've made our reservations for the Yankees game, so keep your glove handy. We're going to see the Yankees play the Red Sox on Wednesday!"

"*Wednesday?* But that's only five days from now! And we always go in early August!"

"Well, that's usually true. But your uncle Louie and aunt Edna are going to Niagara Falls that week with their kids, and it wouldn't be the same without them. The more the merrier, right?" Louie and Edna had five kids, including Zach, their oldest, who was fourteen, and nine-year-old Oscar, the cousin who Derek always had the most fun with.

"But—but what about—" Derek blurted out before catching himself midsentence. He couldn't very well tell her, without checking with her first, that he'd *promised* Dave that he would get to see the Yankees.

Derek knew that his family went to only one Yankees game every summer. It was expensive, not to mention hard to arrange, what with so many cousins and aunts and uncles involved. But they had *always* gone in early August. He'd never even considered that Grandma might change the date.

Now Dave might not get to go to a Yankees game at all, and it would be all Derek's fault.

"Is there some problem, Derek?"

Derek didn't know what to say. He didn't want to seem ungrateful, and he knew it would be too much to ask Grandma to return all those tickets and start over again, making arrangements for twenty-five people to go to another Yankees game, and leaving out Zach and his whole branch of the family just so that Dave could come.

"Derek?"

He opened his mouth to speak, but he never got to say anything, because just at that moment Sharlee came bounding down the stairs, yelling, "Whoopee! Pancakes!"

And at the same moment he heard Aunt Dorien's car pulling into the driveway. Derek realized he'd have to wait till later to talk with Grandma about Dave and the Yankees game.

Which was just as well, because he had no idea what to say or do about it.

Chapter Two

FAMILY FUN

Later that morning, after everyone had their fill of Grandma's pancakes, Derek, Sharlee, Jessica, and Alfie piled into her ancient Oldsmobile, and headed over to the Castle, about a five-minute drive away.

The car was even older than Derek's mom and dad's car, or Grandpa's pickup truck, but Derek loved it anyway. Grandma had driven that same car ever since he could remember. That was one of his favorite things about New Jersey—how everything stayed just the same, summer after summer.

There were already more than a dozen of his cousins running around the big lawn on the property when the car pulled up. Derek got out and started running over to join them. But then he remembered to go back and help Grandma unhook the little ones from their car seats, and help her carry some of the food and drinks she'd brought with her, as her contribution to the daily picnic lunch they all shared while spending their days at the lake.

Derek spotted Oscar, and immediately they started chasing each other around the property, taking turns being the hunter and the hunted. Finally they ended up jumping into the lake off the cement dock, splashing every other kid within ten feet of them.

A few hours later they all sat down for lunch at one of the picnic tables the grown-ups had set up at the edge of the big lawn. Then Zach arrived on his bike, and he and Derek decided to organize a game of Wiffle ball with every kid there.

Wiffle ball was fun, Derek thought, as he told the little ones on his team where to stand, and where to throw the ball if it came to them. But it wasn't the same as playing baseball. After an hour Derek had had more than enough Wiffle ball for one day and was glad when the game ended early, with four of the younger players complaining that they wanted to go swimming. All the kids then made a beeline for the lake. Some jumped right in, but the littler ones lowered themselves down the metal ladder attached to the dock.

Some of the better swimmers swam out to the raft.

The water there was over Derek's head, but he was a pretty good swimmer, as most of the kids were. Growing up at the lake had made them all comfortable in the water.

Derek swam out now and hoisted himself onto the raft with Andrew. Oscar swam up right behind him. Derek helped him up, and they all warmed themselves in the summer sun as they lay on their backs, eyes closed, floating peacefully.

Suddenly Derek heard Sharlee yell, "No! Zach, stop!" He opened his eyes and saw that Zach was standing at the edge of the concrete platform where the property met the lake. He had Sharlee in both his arms, and was about to toss her into the water!

Zach seemed to think that Sharlee was joking, that she really wanted him to throw her in. But Derek knew his sister better. "Hey!" he yelled, cupping his hands over his mouth so that his older cousin could hear him all the way from the raft. "Let her be, Zach. She doesn't want to get thrown in, okay?"

"Aw, come on! It's funny!" Zach called back to him.

"If she doesn't think it's funny, it's not funny," Derek countered, in a tone that didn't allow for any more argument.

Zach seemed disappointed, but he let Sharlee down safely onto the platform. She gave Derek a quick smile and a wave of gratitude. "Thanks," she called to him, and sat back down on the edge of the platform next to Tina and Sophie, two cousins her age.

Meantime, Zach dived in and soon hauled himself up onto the raft beside Derek and the others. "You guys are no fun," he grumbled.

Derek didn't answer. He knew Zach would get over it in a few minutes. Sometimes older kids thought little kids were toys to play around with and goof on. And while Sharlee was not usually timid, she wasn't much for being messed with either.

"That was cool, how you stuck up for your little sister," Oscar said, smiling. "Zach gets on my nerves sometimes too."

"Yeah," Derek said, shrugging. "Big brothers, I guess."

"Not you," Andrew pointed out. "You don't do that to Sharlee."

It was true, Derek had to admit. Oscar and Andrew's admiration made Derek feel good. It was almost like he himself was being a role model to the other kids around him. The thought made him laugh.

"What's so funny?" Oscar asked.

"Nothing," Derek said. But it really was funny how sometimes you were looking for role models. And sometimes you were being one yourself.

That evening, tired from their long, active day at the lake, Derek and Sharlee sat on the porch while Grandma, who never seemed to get tired, made dinner. The sun had already disappeared behind the hill to the west of the house, but across the lake the houses on the east side were still bathed in sunlight. Soon enough Grandpa came home from work and they all sat down to eat.

Afterward, as he did most nights, Grandpa sat down in front of the TV and put his feet up to relax. He was never a big talker, but at the end of a workday, he was too tired to say much of anything. As he watched TV, his eyes started to close, until he realized he was falling asleep and opened them again.

Sharlee sidled over to him and climbed into his lap. "Oh, gosh, have I got to put up with this load of cement sitting in my lap?" he said, making Sharlee giggle.

He pretended to complain about it, but both she and Derek knew he loved having his grandkids around. That was just how Grandpa was. You knew he loved you, even though he never said so.

About fifteen minutes later, though, Grandpa yawned and said, "Listen, some of us have to get up early tomorrow morning. Come on, you sack of potatoes," he told Sharlee. "Off of me, now. There you go."

Sharlee reached out and hugged him before letting him go. Grandpa messed with Derek's hair as he passed Derek on his way to the stairs. "Don't stay up all night, now, big fella," he said.

"I won't, Grandpa," Derek said.

Soon after he'd gone upstairs, Grandma got up from her seat on the couch. "Well," she said, "I'd better get a start on those dishes."

"I'll help!" Derek offered, springing up from his armchair.

"Shhh," Grandma reminded him. "Your grandpa's trying to sleep. Let's not scream too loud, okay?"

Derek put a hand to his mouth. He always forgot to speak quietly after Grandpa had gone to bed. Back at home no one went to bed before nine.

"I'll wash; you dry," Grandma said as she turned on the kitchen faucet.

Sharlee had stayed behind in the living room to watch TV. In the background Derek heard the theme from one of her favorite shows playing, and knew she had changed the channel from the news to cartoons.

Derek was always ready to help Grandma with her work, but he also had another reason for joining her in the kitchen. This was his best chance to bring up the subject that had been gnawing at the back of his mind all day long.

"Um, Grandma?"

"Yes, Derek?"

He hesitated, trying to think of the best way to put the question he wanted to ask. Then he saw the framed picture on the kitchen wall—the one he never got tired of looking at.

It was an old newspaper article with a headline reading FAREWELL TO THE BABE. Below the headline was a black-and-white photograph of a long line of people outside Yankee Stadium. All the men had hats in their hands, but none of them was wearing one on his head.

"Tell me again about how you were there at Babe Ruth's funeral?" he asked his grandma.

"Again?" she asked. "You've only heard that one a hundred times."

"Tell me again," he begged. "Please?"

"Well, I was just a girl, of course. There must have been fifty thousand people there that day, to honor the Babe and say good-bye." She paused, and sighed, remembering that day long ago. "He was the greatest baseball player there ever was, or ever will be."

Then she laughed and gave Derek a sidelong glance. "Of course, there are some people who prefer the Iron Horse—Lou Gehrig. And it's true, he was also one of the greatest players ever—a great teammate who never took a day off, and a wonderful person who never got himself into any kind of trouble—the kind of man any kid would want to grow up to be like."

"A real role model," said Derek, thinking of this afternoon and what had happened with Zach and Sharlee.

"Yes, he was." Grandma paused and sighed. "Still, when you come right down to it, there will never be anyone like the Babe. The greatest player ever, bar none."

She fell silent, and Derek figured it was now or never.

"Grandma, can we go to *another* Yankees game this summer, when Dave is here? I kind of . . . I kind of promised him."

There it was. He felt foolish. Why, oh why, had he promised Dave something he wasn't sure he could make good on?

"Oh, Derek, I don't know," she said, knitting her brows. "It's very expensive to take everybody in the family to a game, and it takes a lot of arranging and scheduling."

"No, I mean just us three—and maybe Sharlee," Derek said. "So that's only four tickets, and we can all go in one car. . . ." He looked up at her hopefully, biting his lip.

"Why didn't you think to ask me in advance?" she asked.

"Sorry, Grandma. I just kind of . . . didn't think of it at the time."

"Well, I don't know. Someone will have to look after the kids while I'm off watching the game . . . but I'll *consider* it."

"Thanks, Grandma!" Derek said, forgetting to keep his voice down, then remembering and covering his mouth with his hand. "Oops. Sorry," he whispered.

"It's a lot to ask, Derek," she said, her face serious, though Derek knew she always had a hard time saying no to him. "I want to think about it for a while first. Just remember, I'm not promising anything—yet."

"Okay," Derek said. "I understand."

He *did* understand. He could only wait, keep his fingers crossed, and hope she'd agree to his plan. Otherwise, what was he going to tell Dave?

Chapter Three

A WHOLE NEW BALL GAME

"Are we there yet?" Sharlee said again, in case anyone hadn't heard her the first three times. She and Derek were sitting in the backseat of Grandma's car as they drove across the George Washington Bridge into New York City.

"Not yet," said Grandma. "But if you look out the window, you can see all the skyscrapers. There's the Empire State Building, with the needle on top."

Sharlee craned her neck. "I see it! I see it!"

Derek smiled. He loved how excited Sharlee always got about things. And today there was plenty to be excited about. They were on their way to Yankee Stadium to watch the Yankees play their archrivals, the Boston Red Sox!

Six other cars were coming too—all filled with Derek's

uncles, aunts, and cousins—twenty-five people in all. Grandma had reserved a whole row in the upper deck in right field for them. It was going to be a blast.

It was only five, and the game didn't start until after seven. None of the other family members' cars had even left New Jersey yet. Derek had talked Grandma into leaving for the stadium at four, ninety minutes earlier than everyone else, so that they could watch the Yankees take batting and fielding practice.

Secretly Derek was hoping that Dave Winfield would even hit one into the upper deck, where Derek could make a fantastic catch and be noticed by the Yankees scouts!

He knew it was just a fantasy. Still, it didn't stop him from dreaming. Most of Derek's dreams were about the Yankees anyway.

As they crossed over the Harlem River into the Bronx, and the stadium loomed in front of them, Grandma said, "By the way, Derek, I've been thinking about your special request. You know the one I mean?"

Of course he did!

"Yes? And?" he asked, leaning forward and biting his lip anxiously.

"What special request?" Sharlee asked, her eyes widening.

"Never mind, nosey," Derek told her, giving her a little tickle that made her squeal with laughter. He hadn't told her about his plans, in case Grandma said no.

"I've decided to allow it—"

"Yesss!"

"*If* you're willing to work to earn the cost of the tickets. If a person wants something extra, he should be willing to work for it."

"What thing?" Sharlee demanded. "What are you *talking* about? Tell me! Tell me!"

Derek laughed. There was no point in trying to hide it from her. She would never stop, he knew, till he told her the big secret, and now that Grandma had agreed, there was no reason not to tell her. "We're going to another Yankees game this summer—me, Dave, Grandma . . . *and* you, of course," he added when he saw that she was about to protest.

"Yay!" Sharlee said, instantly brightening.

"That's if you work for the money to pay for the tickets," Grandma reminded him.

"Uh . . . what kind of work are we talking about?" Derek asked.

"Well, since you're getting so big and strong, I thought you could mow a few lawns. That ought to bring in good money. I'll ask the neighbors up and down the block. Meantime, you can help me with my chores, and with babysitting at the lake."

That didn't sound too hard, Derek thought. As to lawn mowing, he'd never done it before, but how hard could it be? It was only grass, right? "Deal!" he said.

"Good. I suppose you could ask your friend Dave to pay for his own ticket," she added.

"Maybe," said Derek, but he didn't tell her he'd already promised that he'd treat Dave to the game. Derek hadn't figured then on having to pay for three more tickets besides!

While he was considering all this, Grandma had pulled off the highway and onto the streets of the Bronx.

"Why are we going left?" he asked her. "The stadium's the other way!"

"True," said Grandma. "But the cheapest parking lots are *this* way. We'll probably have to walk four or five blocks, but I figure you kids won't mind the exercise."

They parked the car in an outdoor lot, took their shopping bag full of sandwiches with them, and headed off toward the big ballpark. They passed car repair shops, apartment buildings, and baseball-themed restaurants. Overhead the elevated trains of the New York City subway system clattered and shrieked so loudly that they had to hold their ears more than once.

As they approached the stadium, they came to a big, fenced-in park. Well, not a park, really—more of a great big dirt field or sandlot, covering a whole square block, with four baseball diamonds, one in each of its corners.

These "fields" weren't like the ones in Kalamazoo. Back home in Michigan, athletic fields weren't perfect, but they were pretty well taken care of.

Here it was different. There was mostly dirt every-where. There were a few patches of grass in the outfield, looking brown and dead. No one had tended these fields for a long, long time. The chain-link fence surrounding the whole area had holes in it big enough for a grown-up to fit through.

All four fields were occupied—three of them by teen-agers and young adults practicing their hitting and field-ing. But on the nearest field there was a game going on, with full nine-man teams made up of kids who seemed to range in age from eleven—Derek's age—to about fourteen.

Some of the kids were about Derek's size, and some were as big as his cousin Zach. Some were wearing uniform jerseys very much like the ones he'd worn in Kalamazoo, but a lot of these shirts looked too small for the kids wear-ing them. Others wore just T-shirts, even ripped ones.

Derek stopped walking. "Hold on a second," he told Grandma and Sharlee. "I've got to check this out."

The bases were loaded, and the players on his side of the diamond (you couldn't really call it a "dugout," because there were just one or two pieces of wood left on what used to be the benches) were rattling the fence in front of them, yelling for their man to get a hit.

As Derek watched, the other team's pitcher threw a bullet right past the hitter, who swung but hit only air.

On the next pitch the batter hit a screaming liner over the shortstop's head. But at the last moment the kid at short leapt high into the air and snagged the ball in the webbing of his mitt! He then fell flat onto his belly, but, amazingly, he hung on to the ball.

A roar went up from all the other kids on the field—and from Derek, too. It had been an incredible catch, one Derek himself would have been proud to make, and one that he would have dreamed about for weeks afterward.

Suddenly he wished he were out there with those kids, playing in this game, being part of the action.

"What's the score?" he asked the kid nearest to him, on the other side of the chain-link fence.

"It's 5–5," the kid answered, then turned back to the game.

"What inning?"

"Ninth," said the kid without taking his eyes off the action.

"Whoa . . ." Derek was entranced.

"Derek," his grandma said, putting a hand on his shoulder, "are you coming? We'll miss batting practice."

Derek felt suddenly torn. He wanted to see batting practice, all right. He'd brought his mitt with him just in case, hoping against hope that he'd snag a ball. But he also wanted to see what happened next in *this* game right here in front of him.

"Come on, Derek. I want to go get some cotton candy!" Sharlee said impatiently.

"Grandma, can we stay for a few more minutes?" Derek

pleaded. "It's the ninth inning, and I've got to see how this game turns out!"

"Ninth inning? I thought they only play six innings in Little League."

"Yeah, but it's in extra innings!" Derek explained. "It's bases loaded! Pleeease?"

Grandma chuckled and shook her head. "I suppose so," she said. "If Sharlee doesn't mind."

"I *do* mind!" Sharlee said hotly. "I want my cotton candy!"

"Hey, Sharlee," Derek offered, "if we stay for a few minutes, I'll give you half of my giant pretzel, okay?"

Derek always gave her half of it anyway, but the promise seemed to mollify Sharlee. "Okay, but just for five minutes," she said.

So the three of them stood against the fence and watched as the sandlot game went into the tenth inning.

Derek could tell right away that these kids, even the ones his own age and size, were fantastic players. Every one of them was as good as the best players in his league back home. The pitchers threw bullets and didn't walk a lot of batters. The hitters were tough to strike out, and they hit line drives. The fielders snagged those liners like they were easy pop-ups.

Especially the kid at shortstop, the one Derek had first noticed when he'd made that spectacular overhead leap and catch. The others all called him "Jumbo," though he was tiny—even smaller than Derek. The team that Jumbo led—and from the way his teammates looked up to him, it was obvious he was their leader—scored the go-ahead run in the top of the tenth.

Then the other team, which seemed to be led by its catcher, a huge, tough-looking, tough-talking kid with a chipped tooth whom the others called "Tiny"—clearly another joke—tied the score in the bottom of the tenth!

For the next twenty minutes, as the game went on, the teams seesawed back and forth. Even Sharlee stopped complaining as the action drew her in too.

In the eleventh inning the kid in center for Jumbo's team dived for a fly ball he had no chance of catching. He skidded ten feet on the hard ground, while the left fielder retrieved the ball and threw in to second base to hold the runner there.

When the center fielder got up and brushed himself off, Derek saw that his shirt was ripped, and he had cuts on his hands, elbows, and shoulder. But he waved off all offers of help and got right back into position for the next hitter.

"Way to be tough, Pokey!" Jumbo yelled to him, pointing at him with his glove. The kid in center tipped his cap in return.

On the next play a huge argument started over whether a sharp grounder had gone foul or stayed fair. Derek watched as they yelled back and forth about it. In

31

Kalamazoo the umpire would have made a call, and that would have been that. But here there were no umpires. The kids were making the calls themselves.

Finally they decided on a do-over, and everyone calmed down and got back into the game, which remained tied when the hitter struck out to end the frame.

Derek liked these kids. He liked their sense of humor, their baseball skills, their toughness—and, most of all, their passion for the game. On top of it all, they seemed to have so much fun with one another!

Even though Kalamazoo felt like a world away, a small town next to this big city, baseball was the same game. In his own love of baseball, Derek felt close to them. Even though he knew it was impossible, he wished he could somehow get into the game and be in their league.

"Derek, we'd better go now," his grandma said. "The others will be getting there soon, and they'll wonder what happened to us."

"And I'm hungry for my cotton candy—and my pretzel, too," Sharlee added, in case her big brother had forgotten his offer.

"Five more minutes? Pleeeease?" Derek begged. He *had* to see how this game turned out!

But five minutes came and went, with the score still relentlessly knotted. "Come on!" Sharlee demanded. "We're going to miss the national anthem and everything!"

"Really, Derek, it's a quarter to seven," his grandma

added, checking her watch anxiously. "The others will be wondering what became of us."

Derek sighed. "Okay. I guess we *have* to—"

Before he could finish his sentence, the batter fouled a fastball high in the air behind home plate. The ball flew right over the chain-link fence and was coming down toward the curb—where a big, fancy car was parked right in harm's way!

Derek flew into action. Jamming his mitt onto his left hand, he ran toward the spot where the ball was going to land. Leaning as far over the car as he could, he jumped for it, stretching his glove out as far as it would go.

The ball was headed right for the car's windshield and surely would have shattered it. But instead it landed in the webbing of Derek's mitt. He held it up to show everyone that he'd caught it—and was thrilled to hear the sound of all the kids whooping it up, applauding his windshield-saving catch!

"Over here!" Tiny yelled, motioning for Derek to throw it back to him. Afterward he motioned for Derek to come over to the fence.

"Nice catch," said Tiny with a chipped-tooth smile, touching mitts through the chain link as a sort of high five.

Jumbo the shortstop also came over to the fence to introduce himself. "Hey, man," he said to Derek, shaking his head and grinning, "you looked like *me* catchin' that ball!"

"Thanks." Derek could feel his face go red with pleased embarrassment.

"Why don't you come on back next week and get in the game with us?" Jumbo said. "I'll put you on my team. You can hit, can't you?"

"Definitely!" Derek couldn't believe he was actually being invited! "But . . . isn't this some kind of league or something?"

"No, man, not anymore," Tiny said. "It used to be, but a lot of kids couldn't afford it, so it fell apart. But we don't care—we keep playing anyway. Every Wednesday, three o'clock, all summer. Who cares about trophies and uniforms? We just want to keep on playing ball. We can't *not* play."

"We'd be here every day of the week if we could," said Jumbo, "but most of the time the big kids take over everything for themselves." He gestured to the other three fields, where other games were going on, with players no younger than fifteen or sixteen. Then he turned and spat on the ground by his feet.

Derek recoiled slightly. Kids in Kalamazoo didn't spit like that, though he'd certainly seen baseball players do it on TV. It was kind of gross, he thought, but he didn't let it bother him. If these kids were going to invite him to play with them, he wasn't going to pick fights with them. He felt like it would make him a better player if he could pick up some of their skills by watching them, and playing alongside them.

Tiny did say something, though. "Cut that out!" he yelled at Jumbo. "You think spitting makes you look cool? You should see yourself."

"I didn't ask you for advice, man," Jumbo shot back, "so don't be giving it to me, okay?"

Derek thought for a second that they might start fighting, so he interrupted the argument. "That really stinks about not having a league. Every kid who wants to play ball should have one to be in."

"Yeah, well, it's not like that around here," said Jumbo, still looking annoyed but backing off the fight he'd been about to start. "So what do you say, kid? See you next Wednesday, three o'clock?" he asked Derek.

"I'll have to ask my grandma." He gestured toward where she and Sharlee were standing—Sharlee looking more impatient every second. "I don't live around here, see."

"Where you from?" asked Jumbo.

"HEY! YO! Play ball!" yelled one of the kids on the field. Obviously, Sharlee wasn't the only impatient one.

"One second! Pipe down and cool your jets!" Tiny shot back. Somehow he had such respect from everyone there that the other kids all settled down and waited.

"I'm from Michigan," Derek told him. "Kalamazoo. But I'm in Jersey for the summer with my grandparents."

"Kalama—what?" Jumbo said.

"Zoo, man," said Tiny. "You know, as in animals?"

"I've got to go," Derek said. "Sorry—we've got tickets . . ." He nodded toward the stadium across the street.

"You've got Yankees tickets?" Jumbo replied, his eyes going wide. "Man, I wish I could go to a game. I've never been."

"Never?" Derek couldn't believe it. This kid lived right here in the neighborhood.

"Most of us have never been," Tiny said. "It's a lot of moolah."

"Moolah?"

"Money. Cash. Bucks. *Dinero.*"

"Derek!" his grandma called, sounding impatient herself now.

"See you!" Derek said, and took off to join his sister and grandmother. The two kids went back to their game. Derek wondered if he'd ever find out who won, or if he'd ever see them again. He wished he could come back and play with them, and be part of their "league." But how could he ever make that happen?

Anyway, now was not the time to think about that, he figured. It was time to watch baseball at its finest. "Yankees–Red Sox!" Derek said out loud. "It doesn't get any better than this!"

Chapter Four

ON HALLOWED GROUND

As they passed through the turnstile into Yankee Stadium, noise seemed to echo in the air—the sound of thousands of excited people. But Derek was totally silent, taking it all in. So, he noticed, was Grandma. Even Sharlee stood there openmouthed, taking in the chaotic scene.

They rode up three sets of escalators, higher and higher, and then, when they finally emerged through the passageway to the upper deck, they stopped and stared.

The outfield was impossibly green, and huge. Beyond it the infield looked perfect, and the bases shone bright white in the sun. All around them were thousands of people, and the huge video board and scoreboard out in center field were flanked by the bleachers, where the

"Bleacher Creatures" were chanting their cheers loudly.

Derek, Grandma, and Sharlee stared for a long time—until someone waiting behind them in the aisle said, "Uh, excuse me?" They got out of the way, then found their own seats and settled in.

A lot of the seats around them were still empty, partly because of the incredible traffic jam outside, and also because lots of fans were busy buying food and drinks to bring to their seats. Derek figured that was where the rest of his family was right now.

Grandma had a system of her own. She had prepared sandwiches and had brought them in a big shopping bag. They always ate those first. Only after they'd finished their "healthy foods," as Grandma called them, were the kids allowed to spend their food money for the day on popcorn, hot dogs, cotton candy, soda, pretzels, and ice cream.

Grandma and four of Derek's aunts and uncles were the grown-up chaperones for tonight. There were twenty kids with them in all, ranging in age from three to fifteen.

As Derek, Grandma, and Sharlee ate their sandwiches, the Yankees took the field. A roar went up from the crowd, and Derek yelled right along with them. "Woo-hoo!" Sharlee shouted, joining in the excitement.

The game began, with the great Ron Guidry on the mound for the Yanks. Derek could see Rickey Henderson out in center field. Don Mattingly was at first, and Willie Randolph at second.

And there was Dave Winfield right down below him, patrolling right field. Even from way up here, you could tell how big he was—a giant of a man.

Right away the leadoff hitter smacked a screaming line drive that looked like it would be over Winfield's head, but at the last moment he jumped and grabbed it before slamming into the wall!

"Wow! That was awesome! Did you see that?" Derek said, high-fiving his cousin Oscar, who was seated to his left.

"I didn't think he'd ever catch that one!" Oscar said, wide-eyed.

"He's the best!" Derek crowed. "Did you know he was drafted in three sports out of college—baseball, football, and basketball?"

"Really? That's so cool!" Oscar said. "Are you gonna do that too?"

Derek had never considered the question. But he had to admit, it sounded pretty cool. "Sure," he said. "Maybe. Why not?"

The game grew tense in the third inning when, with two outs, the Red Sox offense came to life, helped by a walk, a wild pitch, and a bloop hit. But Guidry pitched his way out of the jam and gave up only one run.

The game remained 1–0 until the seventh, when Don Mattingly singled and Winfield came to the plate. On the 2–2 count, Winfield belted a double to right. Derek heard the ball smack off the wall, although, since the wall was right below him, he couldn't see the ball hit, because his view was blocked by the wall itself.

Mattingly kept going around third base, barreling toward home as the throw came in. It ricocheted off his foot as he slid into the plate, and the Yankees tied the game!

Winfield had taken third base on the throw, and now Derek could see him creeping down the line, trying to make the pitcher nervous.

Sure enough, the pitcher tried to throw behind Winfield and pick him off at third. But the third baseman was off the bag and muffed the catch. When the ball trickled away from him, Winfield turned around and scrambled for home!

"Safe!" Derek screamed, but he couldn't even hear himself amid the roar of the crowd as Winfield popped up and clapped his hands. "We've got this! Yeah!" Derek shouted.

Now it was 2–1, Yanks, and that was how it stayed, because Willie Randolph pulled off an incredible double play to snuff out the Red Sox's last gasp in the ninth.

"New York, New York" played from the loudspeakers as the happy crowd started to file toward the exits.

The whole family packed their bags. They were walking down the long ramps leading down to ground level when Derek thought again about what had happened *before* the game—namely, the invitation those kids at the sandlot had offered him, to come back and play with them next week.

He'd been thrilled and honored to be invited. Those kids were great players, and they'd only seen him make one catch, although Derek had to admit it was one of his best ever. Clearly they thought he could play in their "league," and he wanted to think so too.

But he'd never know unless he got the chance. And how was he going to get Grandma to agree to take him all the way back to the Bronx?

It wasn't like she had a lot of free time.

Derek realized it was a lot to ask, but he wanted so badly to play ball with those kids that he felt he had to try.

He, Grandma, and Sharlee passed the sandlot again on their way back to the car, but the kids he'd watched play had long gone. In their place was a bunch of high-school-aged kids.

Derek waited until they were almost back to the George Washington Bridge before he got up the courage to mention it.

"Grandma," he began, "do you think maybe I could come back next Wednesday and play in a game with those kids?" When she didn't immediately answer, he added, "They invited me!"

"Yes, I did hear that boy invite you, Derek," Grandma said, nodding. From the backseat he couldn't see the expression on her face. "And that was very nice of him. It was a really amazing catch you made there, saving that car's windshield like that."

Derek smiled. But she hadn't answered his question, had she? "So . . . can I come back and play with them?"

"Oh, hon," she said with a sigh, and he could tell that she was about to say no.

But she *didn't*—at least not right then. "Why do you want to come all this way to play ball, when you can play all you want at the lake with your cousins and their friends?"

"Aw, Grandma, it's not the same! I mean, it's fun playing Wiffle ball and teaching the little kids to play catch. But those kids today were better than anybody I've ever played with! It would make me better if I got to play with them, I know it would! I mean, how am I ever going to get good enough to play for the Yankees if I pass up golden opportunities like this?"

"Hmmm," she said.

Derek figured that this was her way of saying no to him, always a very difficult thing for her to do. He slouched down in the backseat in disappointment. Oh, well, it had been a beautiful dream while it had lasted, and he'd always have the memory of that heroic catch, and that invitation.

"You know . . ."

Derek sat up, alert and suddenly hopeful.

"Maybe your aunt Dorien could drive you over there

on her way to work at the hospital. I think she does the afternoon shift on Wednesdays. She could stay with you until Uncle Ernie gets off work at the university. Then he could take over and drive you home." Derek's uncle Ernie worked as a plumbing contractor at Fordham in the Bronx.

"I could ask them both, I suppose," Grandma said softly, almost to herself. Then she glanced sternly over her shoulder at Derek. "But don't go and set your heart on it, Derek. They might very well say no, and I wouldn't want you to have your hopes dashed."

His hopes dashed? But how could he help being hopeful? His dream of playing baseball in the Bronx was alive—at least for today!

Chapter Five

WORKER BEE

Derek was a man on a mission. Grandma had said he could go to the Yankees game with Dave if he did whatever jobs she gave him between now and then. Well, this was his first job, and he was determined to show her what kind of worker he was!

He had laid out twenty-four pieces of bread and was spreading the peanut butter and jelly, piece by piece. The sandwiches would feed all the kids down at the lake when they got hungry for lunch.

Derek had always been good about doing his chores back at home. It was a big part of the contract he'd signed with his parents, which laid down all the rules he had to abide by.

In fact, everyone in Derek's whole family was a hard worker. His parents were holding down two jobs each this summer, to help earn extra money so he and Sharlee could take part in all the class trips and extracurricular activities they loved.

His grandparents, aunts, and uncles were all hard workers, so he didn't mind having to earn the price of the Yankees tickets he wanted. Even Sharlee had chores, though she was still little. It seemed to Derek that they'd both had chores ever since they could walk.

"Derek, don't you think that's a lot of peanut butter for one sandwich?" Grandma asked. Derek looked down at the peanut butter that was dripping off the edge of the bread like a gooey waterfall.

"Oops. Sorry," he said.

"What's on your mind this morning?" she asked. "Not making sandwiches, I guess." She shot him a crooked grin and a wink.

"I was just"—he scooped up the extra peanut butter on the edge of his knife and used it on the next piece of bread—"you know, thinking about taking Dave to—"

"To the Yankees game. I thought so," she said. "Well, let's see. You've made how many sandwiches so far?"

Derek counted them up. "Eight."

"And we need twelve. So keep working," she said, teasing him. "Those tickets don't come cheap."

Derek heard a car pulling into the driveway. "It's Aunt

Dorien!" he said excitedly, recognizing the sound of her car. "Grandma, don't forget to ask her about—"

"I know, I know," she said, holding up a hand. "Don't think for a minute that I forgot about it."

He quickly finished making the last sandwiches, then ran outside so that he didn't miss anything.

"Well, let me see, now," Aunt Dorien was saying as she fished a datebook out of the giant purse she carried every-where she went. You never knew what she would pull out of that bag. One time, Derek remembered, she'd pulled out a big old turtle she'd found crossing the road, because she wanted to put it back in the woods where it belonged.

"I have a Wednesday afternoon shift," she said. "Got to be at the hospital by four. What time does he have to be there?"

"The game's at three," Derek volunteered.

"I could get him there and stay till three thirty," Aunt Dorien said, "but then I'd have to go, and who'd be there to watch Derek and get him home? I don't get off work till eight."

"I thought maybe Ernie could get over there," said Grandma. "He'll be back home later, and I'll see if he's okay with it."

"Well, I am if he is," Aunt Dorien said with a smile.

"Thanks, Aunt Dorien!" Derek ran to hug her, and she laughed.

"Hey, I haven't done anything yet!" she protested.

That was how the whole family was, always ready to

help one another out. And with so many kids running around all over the place, they had to be!

"Derek!" his grandma said, pointing. "Go make sure Alfie doesn't wander off too near the road!"

Alfie had slipped out of the car and had begun stumbling in the general direction of the road. Derek hustled after him and caught him, feeling vaguely guilty. He knew he was supposed to be keeping an eye on all the kids today, as part of his work for Grandma. Now he'd gotten off to a bad start. But he'd been so intent on hearing what the grown-ups were saying!

Derek told himself to be more careful from now on.

"No, Deirdre, don't hit Tommy!" Derek heroically tried to separate the two four-year-olds, both of whom seemed ready to go to war over who was going to play with the robot toy Tommy was now holding. "Allie, no! Don't run over there. There's poison ivy!"

Leaving both combatants behind, Derek raced to the edge of the property by the woods, where seven-year-old Allie was about to get herself into a world of itchy torment by chasing her soccer ball into a patch of the nasty weeds.

Wow. Taking care of kids is harder than I thought! Derek said to himself, gently leading Allie away from the edge of the woods. Then he went in after the ball himself, using a long stick to get it out of the troublesome spot, before kicking it back out into play.

He'd been "on duty" since ten o'clock that morning, and

it was now almost four in the afternoon. Soon some of the aunts and uncles would be showing up after work to pick up their kids and take them home. Most lived in or near Greenwood Lake.

Also coming home from work would be those grown-ups who lived here at the Castle, in its large apartments, or in one of the other buildings on the property. They would include Uncle Ernie, whose return Derek was keeping an eye out for.

Ernie was one of Derek's favorite uncles. He was always ready to be one of the kids and play with them, chasing the little ones around like a big goofy monster, or teaching them how to throw and catch a ball. He had been one of Derek's earliest fans.

Derek still remembered the time when Uncle Ernie had bought him his first Yankees cap. It was way back when he was only five and had just moved to Michigan with his mom, dad, and Sharlee.

Derek figured it was because Ernie didn't want him to forget where he'd come from, or which team he should always, always root for. Either way, it sure had worked. Derek was a huge Yankees fan, even though his own dad rooted for the hometown Tigers.

Of course, Grandma could also take a lot of the credit for Derek's love of the Yankees, with her never-ending stories about Babe Ruth, Joe DiMaggio, Yogi Berra, and Mickey Mantle.

Here came Uncle Ernie now, pulling into the driveway in his big red pickup truck! Derek raced over to meet him, keeping one eye on his cousins to make sure they weren't getting into trouble.

"Well!" said Ernie as Derek raced up to greet him. "I knew we were best buds, but you sure are excited to see me today!"

"You're the best, Uncle Ernie!"

"I am? What'd I do now?" Ernie asked, scratching his head in mock confusion.

"You're going to come and watch me play ball in the Bronx next Wednesday, and take me home after! At least, I *hope* you are. . . ."

Derek hadn't been able to contain himself and had blurted the whole thing out just like that, without using any of the careful preparation he'd practiced all day long.

But it didn't matter. Once he'd told Ernie the whole story, his uncle nodded, stroked his chin, and said, "I don't see why I couldn't get down there by three thirty." With a shrug he added, "Long as Dorien can hang with you till then, we'll be okay."

Derek threw his arms around Ernie, and said, "Thankyouthankyouthankyou!"

"Hey! Hey, don't get all mushy, now!"

"So . . . we're on for Wednesday?" Derek asked, just to make sure there was no misunderstanding.

"You got it, big fella," said Ernie, clapping him on the shoulder. "Anything that gets you closer to playing at Yankee Stadium, count me in."

Derek felt like he'd just been dropped off in heaven! Thanks to his fantastic aunt Dorien and his stupendous uncle Ernie—who'd always been big believers in Derek's dream of playing for the Yankees—he was going to get to play ball with the best players he'd ever been around!

Chapter Six

WHISTLE WHILE YOU WORK

"So, how are you holding up? Ready for some more work?"

"Sure, Grandma," Derek said as he helped her dry the dishes after dinner Friday evening. "Whatever it takes!"

"Okay, then," she said, drying her hands on a dish towel. Putting an arm around his shoulder, she led him to the kitchen table, where they both sat down. "I've got three neighbors lined up, and you can mow all their lawns tomorrow." Grandma checked the items off on a list she'd made. "When you get back, you can help me with the laundry. And *then*—"

"Wait, there's *more*?"

"You said you wanted to work, didn't you?" Grandma asked. "And," she went on, "it turns out that Charlie

Detweiler's family is going on vacation starting this week-end, so he needs somebody to cover his paper delivery route on Sunday morning. His mom says he'll come over late tomorrow afternoon and explain everything to you. You can use your old bike to get around, if it's not already too small for you—or you can borrow his if you need to."

"No, mine's fine," said Derek. He'd never delivered newspapers before, but it sounded like fun, and anything that involved bike riding was okay with him.

"Good. I'll phone them back and tell them you're good to go."

"Is that it?" Derek asked, getting out of the chair. There was a TV program on in the living room, and he could hear Sharlee giggling away at whatever was so funny.

"That's all I've got for *now*," she said. "Remember, though, if you want something badly enough, you've got to be willing to work hard to get it. Those tickets aren't free, you know."

"I know, Grandma," Derek said, giving her a hug and a kiss before heading for the living room. "Thanks."

He sat down on the couch next to his little sister, and laughed with her at the antics of people and animals in funny home videos on the TV show.

But inside he was thinking way ahead. Those jobs Grandma had lined up for him sounded like they'd be a breeze. After all, biking was one of his favorite things to do. And how hard could mowing a lawn be, anyway?

Besides, the reward at the other end was huge. Not only was he going to get to play with those kids in the Bronx next week, but he was also going to get to treat his best friend Dave to his very first major-league baseball game!

Whew!

Derek paused and wiped the sweat off his forehead. He'd been pushing the lawn mower around this yard for fifteen minutes, and already his shirt was half-soaked, and his eyes stung from the beads of sweat that had trickled into them.

The two lawns he'd already mowed were fairly small, and he'd done them at warp speed, just to get the jobs over with, so that he could have some swimming time down at the lake later in the day.

This third lawn was much bigger, though, and just as bumpy and rocky as the other two but with higher grass, and lots of little nooks and crannies that made him have to keep turning the lawn mower this way and that.

He paused and took a drink of water from the bottle Grandma had given him. "Don't forget to keep drinking water," she'd told him. "I don't want you getting heatstroke."

Derek didn't know what heatstroke was, but now, in the noonday sun, after two hours of racing around lawns, back and forth and back and forth, he was ready for a break.

He looked around. Two thirds of the yard had yet to be touched. Derek decided he could just jam it and finish in record time, no matter how out of breath he got or how fast his heart beat. He decided to time himself, counting silently, betting that he could finish the lawn before he counted to five hundred.

Twenty minutes later he was done. The lawn was mowed, at the count of 475. He'd cleaned off the mower and put it back into the neighbor's garage, and thanked her when she'd paid him for his work. The second the door was shut behind her, he blew out a breath and wiped his brow, glad to finally be finished!

He ran half the way back home but had to stop and take another drink from the water bottle, emptying it this time. His side hurt from running, and his ears popped so that his heavy breathing sounded really loud inside his head.

Wow, he thought. *Maybe I should slow it down a little next time.*

He was tired at the end of his labors, but at least nothing hurt except for that stitch in his side. By late afternoon, though, that had changed. When Charlie Detweiler came over to show him the ins and outs of newspaper delivery, Derek's arms and legs had already stiffened up and were sore as could be, and his feet were hot and throbbing.

Derek was glad that his next jobs were doing laundry

and delivering papers. Those tasks sounded like a snap after mowing three lawns in one day. Besides, the jingle of money in his pockets reminded him of why he was doing it all.

He couldn't wait for Dave to get here!

It was only eight in the morning, but the day was already getting hot. Derek's legs, still sore from yesterday's lawn mowing, kept pumping, willing the old bicycle up the long hill.

Funny how he'd never even noticed that the road had this gradual slope. It wasn't a steep hill, but it just kept going, and going, and *going*. Derek had to stand up and put all his weight into pedaling before he finally got to the top.

This paper route, while he'd enjoyed it a lot for the first half hour or so, was getting to be a long slog. He'd done as Charlie had suggested, breaking the route down into two parts. The first part was a set of streets with lots of houses that got the paper. All Derek had to do was cycle by the front of the house and toss a paper onto the front walkway. If there was a long driveway, he would cycle in and back out, but he never had to stop the bike—just develop a rhythm of cycling and tossing.

This second part of the route, however, was different. It went out to the edges of town, where the houses were far apart and there were more hills. Once, he misread the map Charlie had given him, and it took him ten minutes of cycling around in circles to find the right address.

Derek tossed his last paper out of the bike's basket and headed for home, happy to be done with his latest job. His legs felt like lead, and his right arm felt like it was about to fall off from flinging so many newspapers!

Why was it, he wondered, that playing ball never made him achy and tired, but working did? His energy flagging fast, he made it home, stowed the bike away, and collapsed onto the sofa, ready to relax at last.

Oh, well. At least he had made a good start on the money he needed. But it was going to take a lot more work to pay for those Yankees tickets. And with the lawns cut and the papers delivered, where else was he going to earn money?

"How'd it go?" Grandma asked, seeing him sprawled on the sofa. "Did you rake in big bucks this morning?"

"It was okay," said Derek. "Tiring."

"Well, I hope you're ready for more tomorrow," she chirped. "I found you three more lawns to mow! Isn't that dandy?"

"Awesome," Derek managed to say, without much excitement.

"Well, then," she said, pleased. "Feel like a game of catch before lunch?"

"Aw, Grandma," said Derek, shifting his aching legs on the couch, "I'm too pooped right now. Maybe later, okay? Or tomorrow . . . after lawn mowing?"

"Well! That's a switch," she said. "Usually I'm the one who's tired, and you're the one who's rarin' to go!"

He smiled but didn't have the energy to laugh with her. Never before in his life had he turned down a game of catch!

Chapter Seven
HE WORKS HARD FOR THE MONEY

Dinner on Monday evening was quieter than usual, although Sharlee kept up her usual end of the conversation, telling them excitedly about all the things that had happened to her that day: ". . . and we found this caterpillar and it was so beautiful, but then Oscar put it on Jessica's head and she freaked out, and . . ."

Grandma laughed at Sharlee's antics, but Derek, who usually joined in the laughter, could only muster an occasional nod and a smile. He was just too tired to exhaust himself laughing. Looking over at Grandpa as he ate his meal, slowly and silently Derek thought he totally understood how Grandpa felt.

Grandpa enjoyed listening to Sharlee's stories too. He

just didn't show it in the same way. When she didn't get the response she wanted from him, she started to climb up onto his lap while he was trying to put his napkin on it.

"Hey, you little rascal, you. I'm trying to eat here. Look out, or I might eat you by mistake." He pretended to try to eat her, and she burst into giggles and snuck a kiss before running away in mock fright.

"These kids today," he said, shaking his head and pretending to disapprove. "They think they can just kiss anybody they want."

After dinner they watched TV for a little while, just as they did most nights. Grandma asked Sharlee if she wanted to help with the dishes tonight instead of Derek. "I think you're old enough to do it now, don't you?" she asked Sharlee.

"I am totally old enough," Sharlee said, half-insulted that Grandma would think anything else. "Come on, I'll show you!"

After the two of them had gone into the kitchen, Derek let himself stretch out into the half-lying-down position Grandpa always wound up in before dozing off in front of the tube.

Grandpa opened one eye and saw what Derek was up to. He closed it again, and Derek thought he might have fallen asleep. But then Grandpa said, eyes still closed, "So, your grandma tells me you've been out doing some odd jobs, huh?"

"Uh-huh," Derek said, sighing.

"Looks like you tired yourself right out," said Grandpa, lifting his head to give Derek a careful look-over. "Must have been some job you got yourself."

"Just mowing lawns," Derek said. "And delivering papers. And running after the little kids, and helping Grandma, and—"

"That's a lot of jobs," Grandpa said. "I guess you think you worked pretty hard, huh?"

"Uh-huh."

"That's good. Hard work never hurt anybody."

"I don't know, Grandpa. It hurts pretty good right now."

"Ha!" Grandpa nodded his head. "Well, then maybe I ought not to mention . . ."

"Mention what?" Derek sat up on the couch. Anything with a note of mystery and surprise to it always got his attention.

"Oh, nothing. . . . You're probably not up to it anyway."

"Come on, Grandpa! Tell me!" Derek begged.

Grandpa folded his arms across his stomach and looked at Derek as if he were sizing him up. "Your grandma tells me you're trying to earn money for Yankees tickets, is that right?"

"Yes!"

"Well, I thought I might let you come to work with *me* one day. Help me out here and there. Earn yourself some more of that money. But if you're not up to it—"

"Yes! I want to! Can I, Grandpa? Can I?"

"I don't know," said Grandpa, sitting up and stretching his bones as if they ached even worse than Derek's. "I'm not sure you can take work that's *really* hard."

"I can! I can take it!" Derek insisted. Anytime he was challenged, his competitive streak automatically kicked in.

Grandpa looked at him without saying anything for a long time—maybe ten seconds.

"Well?" Derek asked.

Grandpa sighed. "All right, then. I've got a couple of things that need doing over at the church that you ought to be able to handle."

"Great! When can I come with you?"

"Well, it's already too late for you to get up at four thirty tomorrow morning. You've got to make sure you get yourself a good night's sleep the night before, because you're going to need it. And I've got to do roofing Wednesday, so that doesn't work. Can't have you going up there. How about Thursday?"

Derek was thrilled. He couldn't believe that Grandpa had actually invited him to come to work with him! As far as Derek knew, none of the other kids in the family had ever been invited. He was also glad Grandpa didn't invite him for Wednesday. That was the day he was going to play ball in the Bronx!

Although he was honored to be going to work with Grandpa, he was also a little nervous about what he'd meant by "*really* hard work." Well, whatever it was, Derek was determined to prove that he could do it.

By Wednesday, Derek felt like a completely different person. His legs, back, and hands had stopped hurting altogether, and his energy had come roaring back.

He was so excited that he could barely sit still—and if not for the seat belt holding him in place, he would have been bouncing off the insides of Aunt Dorien's car.

Was she driving incredibly slowly on purpose? Or was it just that Derek was so eager to get to the Bronx? Either way, this ride was taking forever!

One thing he did notice for sure—the muscles in his arms were bigger than they'd been the week before. That had to be from pushing lawn mowers around and throwing newspapers onto front porches from a moving bicycle.

For this occasion he'd put on his favorite Yankees jersey—the pin-striped one with the number 31 on the back, and the name "WINFIELD" arching over the number.

"There's the stadium now! The field is over that way!" Derek pointed, directing his aunt to turn at the next intersection. "This is how Grandma went," he added, in case she didn't believe him.

She turned left and drove up to the sandlot field. "Wow, I didn't even know this was here!" Aunt Dorien said as she drove past. "And where did Grandma park the car?"

"Keep on going." It was another couple of blocks to the

parking lot, and once they got out, Derek practically raced back toward the ball field—except he had to stop and wait for Aunt Dorien to catch up. She was pretty slow, even for a grown-up.

The kids were already there, throwing the ball around and shagging flies in the outfield. "You go on and get into the game," Aunt Dorien told him, giving him a pat on the back. "I'm just going to sit here on this bench and watch, till Uncle Ernie shows up."

"Thanks, Aunt Dorien—and thanks for doing this! You're the best!"

"Oh, yeah, that's what they all say," she said with a laugh. "That's me, all right."

Derek knew she was only joking. But he also knew that everyone *did* say that about Aunt Dorien. She must have been a great nurse, because she was always doing stuff for other people, just to be nice.

Grateful, excited, and also unexpectedly nervous, Derek jogged around to the gap in the fence.

Tiny was hitting balls to the infielders before the game. Derek saw Jumbo out at shortstop make a diving stop on a sharp ground ball. Derek waved, and Jumbo waved back. "Hey, look who's here, you guys!" Jumbo said.

"Heeey!" said Tiny, welcoming Derek with a high five. "Glad you decided to come back and play."

Some of the other kids gathered around. Derek noticed that not all of them looked friendly. "Who's this kid? He's not from around here," said one, looking Derek over.

"Besides, where are we gonna put him?" one of the others asked. "We've already got enough kids!"

"Never mind, T-Bone," Tiny told him. "This guy can play. He's the one who saved that car from the foul ball last week. Remember?" Turning to the kid who had objected, he said, "Besides, he came all the way from—where?"

"New Jersey," Derek said. "Greenwood Lake."

"No, not there. That other place you said . . ."

"Oh. You mean Kalamazoo."

"Yeah, that's it! All the way from Kalamazoo!" Tiny said. "Wherever that is."

"Michigan," Derek told him.

"And what's your name again?"

"Derek. Derek Jeter." He offered his hand, and Tiny grabbed it and gave it a shake.

"Now you all just chill," Tiny told the others. "Derek here can play short center till Yo-yo leaves to babysit his sister. Then he can move to right."

Yo-yo? T-Bone? These kids all had such cool nicknames! Derek wondered what, if anything, they'd wind up calling *him*—if he played well enough to get invited back a second time, that is.

Chapter Eight
GETTING INTO THE GAME

Derek was out in short center field—a strange position, since it doesn't officially exist in any baseball league. In fact, if these kids had still had a league, he wouldn't have had this chance. So he was grateful and excited just to be here, short center or not.

One thing about playing this position, he knew, was that you were going to get a lot of balls hit to you. Any grounder to second or short that got through the infield, you had a chance to make a play on. Any shallow fly ball, to left, right, or center, was in his range.

He was going to have plenty of chances to impress these kids. All he had to do was not blow it.

He could tell that this "league" had an unspoken

rule—only really good players got to be in the games. It was going to be a challenge to keep up, especially because some of these kids were older, and bigger.

Jumbo was on his team, at shortstop. So Derek would also have a close-up view of every move he made. And that was important to Derek, because he wasn't here just to impress these kids. More than anything else, he wanted to improve his own game.

Tiny was on the opposing team today, catching, as he had been last week. Derek watched as Tiny gathered his team around him. Tiny and Jumbo were the two captains, and both of them were natural leaders. Derek could tell by the way all the other kids hung on every word they said.

Derek waved to his aunt Dorien, and she gave him a big thumbs-up, then clapped a couple of times and yelled, "Go, Derek!"

He smiled, though he did feel just a little embarrassed. He was the newest kid there, and the only one with a fan club.

The game began, with Derek's team in the field. T-Bone, the other team's leadoff man, quickly hit an infield single— even though Jumbo nearly caught him at first base with a desperate, off-balance throw.

Jumbo seemed upset with himself for not playing the ball better, though Derek couldn't see how anyone else could have even made that play close.

GETTING INTO THE GAME

T-Bone soon stole second, on the pitch that struck out the number-two man. Next up was a tall, thin kid who looked like he could hit a ball right through a brick wall. On the first pitch to him, he cracked a rocket straight at Derek!

Derek froze for a split second, being unfamiliar with playing this weird position. Then, realizing how hard the ball had been hit, and seeing how it was going to go over his head, he raced backward and timed his leap.

"Yaaah!" he yelled as he reached out in midair and snagged it. Then he fell into a somersault as he hit the ground. As soon as he came up, he turned and fired the ball to second.

Jumbo caught it and tagged the runner out before he could get back to the base. *Double play! Inning over!*

Derek could hear Aunt Dorien whooping it up from her seat on the bench. His teammates were shouting their surprised congratulations and slapping him on the back with their mitts as they headed back to their side of the diamond.

"Yo, yo, yo!" said the kid called Yo-yo, giving Derek a double high five. Derek laughed, understanding at once how Yo-yo had gotten his nickname.

"Nice play, kid," said Jumbo, giving him a little nod. "What'd you say your name was again?"

"Derek."

"Well, Derek, that was some play. That's *two* now. I

67

guess you can play the field some. But I don't know if you can hit. So I'm going to bat you tenth for today, all right? I don't want anybody getting upset about the new kid taking his spot. You've got to prove yourself first, understand?"

Derek nodded. Of course he understood. He was the stranger here, and he had to earn everything he got. So he stood in front of the bench and watched as his teammates built momentum, with a leadoff walk followed by a double to left by Jumbo.

Tiny took off his mask and signaled to the outfielders to shift, because the next hitter was a lefty and, apparently, a pull hitter. The fielders obeyed his signs without question.

Was it just Tiny's talent as a ballplayer? Or his size? Or the way he ordered his teammates around? Or was there something else about Tiny that made the other kids respect him?

With the runners at second and third, the batter up hit a fly ball to center. Both runners tagged up, and the throw came in to home plate just ahead of the first runner.

Tiny caught it and blocked the plate. As Derek watched in shock, the runner slammed right into Tiny, trying to make him drop the ball!

Tiny fell over backward, hitting his head on the hard dirt. He lay there, but held up the ball to show that the runner was out. Then, while Tiny was down, Jumbo took advantage of the situation by trying to score all the way from second base!

Tiny realized what was happening, but it was too late. Jumbo slid, keeping his body on the other side of the plate and reaching out to touch it with his fingertips.

Tiny reached over to tag him but couldn't quite reach that far.

"Safe!" Jumbo yelled, getting up and clapping his hands. "Yeah, baby!" He spat a few times on the dirt. Derek wondered if that was Jumbo's answer to Tiny's giving him a hard time about spitting last week.

Seeing that Tiny was still down on the ground, Derek bent over and helped him get up. "You okay?" he asked.

"Yeah, man. Thanks." Tiny shook his head a few times, took a few deep breaths, and put the mask back on. "That's two outs," he called to his fielders. "Let's go!"

"What'd you help him up for, man?" Jumbo asked Derek afterward. He spat again, twice. "He's on *their* team."

Again Derek didn't know what to say. He'd never have thought about *not* helping somebody up who might be hurt—even if they were on the other team.

Tiny's team, inspired by his toughness and grit, shut Jumbo and Derek's team down after that.

In the third inning Jumbo made two run-saving catches to keep the score 1–0. One catch was so amazing that Derek determined to try and perfect it himself, by practicing it back in New Jersey.

The ball in question was hit to Jumbo's right. He had to go a long way at full speed to grab it, and Derek thought he had no chance to throw the runner out at first.

But somehow Jumbo had leapt into the air and twisted his body around at the same time, allowing him to get off a good strong throw without having to come to a complete stop and brace his back foot before he threw.

Jumbo's other great play was even more amazing. It was a foul fly ball up the third-base line. Jumbo started out a mile away from it, but he went full speed from the get-go, ran straight for the chain-link fence, leapt two feet into the air, and snagged the ball. His momentum carried him right up the fence, so that he was hanging on to it like a monkey with one hand—but he held out the other with the ball in his mitt to show that he'd made the catch for the third out of the inning!

Wow! thought Derek. He'd never seen anybody go after a foul ball like that. But even though he was amazed, he knew that he too cared that much about winning.

One day, he said to himself, *I'm going to make a play like that.*

Finally, in the bottom of the third, Derek came to bat for the first time, with a man out and nobody on base. He'd been watching the opposing pitcher for two innings now, and he'd studied the kid's speed, the movement of his pitches, and the kinds of pitches he liked to throw. Derek knew that he featured a sizzling fastball and a slow, devastating curveball that dived straight down.

But Derek had also noticed that the pitcher seemed to

make a scary face every time he threw the curve. Derek guessed it was to make the hitters think a fastball was coming, and so fake them out.

He decided to wait for the scary face, then wallop the curveball. He let two fastballs go by, both for strikes. He sure hoped the pitcher would throw him a curve in this at bat, because it was going to be hard for Derek to make solid contact with that fastball. It was faster than any he'd ever faced in Little League.

Derek fouled off two more heaters before the pitcher finally made his scary face. Derek held back for a split second, then swung for the opposite field. He hit the ball solidly between the first and second basemen, and then he took off like a shot.

The ball had so much backspin that it skidded right past the right fielder, who had been playing shallow, underestimating Derek's hitting ability. Derek never broke stride but kept on going, shooting for second!

And when he saw the throw was coming into second way too late, he just kept on going, heading for third!

When the second baseman realized what Derek was up to, he wheeled and rushed his throw to third. It sailed over the third baseman's head and bounced off the chain-link fence into left field.

Derek, who'd slid into third, got right back up and alertly headed home, and scored easily!

His teammates whooped and hollered and shook the

chain-link fence as hard as they could. *No wonder it's all bent out of shape,* thought Derek as he received their high fives and back slaps.

He looked over to wave to Aunt Dorien but saw that Uncle Ernie had arrived and taken her place. Ernie pointed at Derek, as if to say, *Attaboy!* Derek smiled and tipped his Yankees cap.

"So listen here," said Jumbo, coming up to him as the next hitter was busy striking out. "What position do you usually play?"

"Uh . . . short," said Derek, not sure if he'd made a mistake in revealing the truth.

"Hah!" Jumbo replied with a little laugh. "That's funny. Well, I guess you and I are going to be on opposite sides from now on, huh?"

Derek couldn't believe it! Not only was Jumbo telling him he was welcome to come back again next time, but he was also saying that Derek would get to play shortstop!

The rest of the game flew by in a blur. Derek was floating on a cloud, and playing with confidence. He singled, stole a base (although he didn't score), and made a couple of easy catches after taking over for Yo-yo in right field.

The score stayed 2–0, and that was how the game ended, on another incredible play by Jumbo.

With two out and men on first and third, the hitter made solid contact with a fastball. The ball was hit straight up the middle, almost directly over second base. Jumbo, who had been playing over toward third, had an incredibly long way to go to get anywhere near it.

Derek, in right field, had been prepared to back up the play and make sure the ball didn't get away, allowing the runner at first to scoot over to third. But there was no doubt in his mind that it was at least a single and that a run would score. That would cut the lead in half and leave men at first and second as the tying and winning runs, with the cleanup hitter coming to bat.

But none of that actually happened. Somehow, some way, Jumbo managed to get to the ball, diving headlong. Then he flipped the ball behind him, straight out of his mitt, to the second baseman for the force out.

Game over!

The team went wild, all of them surrounding Jumbo, their captain and hero. Derek cheered too. Jumbo was exactly the kind of player Derek wanted to be. He was a real role model.

True, Derek had been taken aback when Jumbo spat on the ground, and when he'd criticized Derek for helping Tiny up. But now Derek put his doubts aside. After all, Jumbo was the best shortstop he had ever played with. If Derek wanted to play for the real Yankees someday, he knew he would first have to be able to do the kinds of things he'd seen Jumbo do today.

He promised himself he would work on each of those plays, from now on until he'd mastered them—all except going up the fence, of course. You couldn't practice that, after all.

"Yo, yo, man!" said Yo-yo, slapping Derek five. "You coming back next week?"

"I . . . I think so," Derek said, not really sure he'd be able to.

"Good game, Jersey," said Tiny, who'd taken off his catching gear and was mingling with the whole crew now, not just his own team. "You play pretty smart, for a little kid."

"I'm not a little kid!" Derek protested, even though he figured Tiny was just ribbing him.

"Next to me you are. How old did you say you were?"

"Eleven."

"Yeah, well, I'm almost thirteen, so there you go. Anyway, you coming back next time?"

"I'm going to try," Derek said truthfully. "But the thing is, even if I can get here next time, my friend is going to be visiting the week after that, and if I came then, he'd have to come too."

"Uh-huh." Tiny thought for a moment, frowning. "Can he play?"

"Oh yeah!" Derek assured him. "He can play."

Derek felt a *little* bit dishonest. Even though Dave was pretty good for Little League in Kalamazoo, Derek wasn't really sure he could stand up to the level of play here. Still, he would have said anything at all if it meant he and Dave could get into a game here together!

"Okay. I guess it'll be all right. Bring him along, and we'll fit him in somehow. Short center, maybe."

"Thanks, Tiny!" Derek said, shaking hands before saying good-bye to the whole gang and jogging over to where Uncle Ernie was waiting for him.

On the way home Derek thought a lot about the best-played baseball game he'd ever been in.

And he'd kept up! No, he'd *more* than held his own. On top of it all, he'd scored an invitation for next week, and one for both him and Dave the week after!

That is, assuming all the grown-ups were down with the plan.

Derek thought about Tiny and Jumbo, how they each carried themselves, on and off the field. They were both leaders but in totally different ways. Jumbo led by his spectacular talent on the field, and his mischievous, magnetic personality.

Tiny, while he was a great player too, led more by his toughness behind the plate, and his kindness with the other kids. He would never, Derek was sure, do anything like spitting on the dirt, or not helping an opposing player up off the ground.

"Great game, huh?" Uncle Ernie said, glancing at Derek in the rearview mirror.

"Oh yeah," Derek said.

"Aunt Dorien said you made a heck of a play in the first inning. Sorry I missed that one."

Uncle Ernie had always been a big baseball fan. He loved to listen to Derek talk about his dream of playing for the Yankees. "That must have been exciting for you, huh, kid? Playing in the shadow of the stadium itself?"

"I guess," Derek said. He didn't want to sound too excited.

"Well! Aren't you Mr. Cool now? You know, I see right through you." They both laughed. "It's okay. I was super-excited just to watch you play. You've come a really long way since last year."

"You think so?" Derek tried not to show how pleased he was.

"No doubt," said Uncle Ernie, edging the car through afternoon rush-hour traffic heading back over the bridge to New Jersey. "So . . . you playing again next week?"

"If you can come and take me home. And if Aunt Dorien or somebody can drive me there. And if Grandma says it's okay."

"Something tells me it's all going to happen just like that," said Ernie. "Is there anybody in this family who can say no to you when you get your mind set on something? Anyhow, you can count me in. I'm off work same time next week."

They drove home to Greenwood Lake, and Derek got out of the car. "Thanks, Uncle Ernie! You're the best!" he said as he waved good-bye.

"How was it?" Grandma asked when he came inside.

"Awesome!" Derek replied, giving her a big hug. "And they invited me for next week! And they said Dave could play too!"

"Whoa. Hold on, now, Derek!" said Grandma. "Let's not get ahead of ourselves. Your friend's not coming till next Friday, so he won't be here in time for the next game. Anyway, we'll have to get his parents' permission, I think. Staying here with us at the lake is one thing. Spending time in the city, with kids we don't know, being supervised by relatives that Dave's *parents* don't know . . . Yes, we'll have to run it by them."

Derek bit his lip. Dave's parents were very protective of him. Would they allow him to play ball with older kids from the big city?

Derek sure hoped so. He couldn't wait to tell Dave the good news!

Chapter Nine

A DEAL IS A DEAL

"Hi, Mom! Hi, Dad!"

"Hey, how's it going back east?" his mom asked.

"Awesome!" Derek told her. "You won't believe what happened today!" He cradled the phone between his ear and his shoulder because both his hands were busy drying dishes.

"Oh, put those down," Grandma said in a hushed tone. "You can finish later."

Derek dried his hands and went on filling his parents in on all the news. "I got to play baseball in the Bronx today!"

"Oh? Yes, Grandma told us about those kids inviting you," his mom said.

"How'd it go?" asked his dad.

"It was the best game I ever played in! Dad, you should see these kids. They can do amazing stuff—all of them! Especially this kid Jumbo! He's a shortstop! And he said I can play short for the other team next week, if I get permission to come."

"Again?" said his mom. "Oh, Derek, that's asking a lot of Ernie and Dorien."

"The Bronx is far away," said his dad, "and your aunt and uncle are busy people. They can't always be getting you in and out of the city."

"But if they said yes?" Derek said in a pleading tone.

There was a short silence on the other end of the line. "What does Grandma say?" asked his mom.

Derek held out the phone, and Grandma took it. She listened, then said, "Ernie says everyone behaved themselves. . . . Oh, I'm sure they don't mind. They're big fans of his, you know. . . . They said he held his head up just fine with all those kids, yes. And some of them were older than him too! . . . Well, I'll let you talk to him." She handed the phone back to Derek.

"Your grandma seems to think it's okay, you playing over there," said his dad.

"So long as someone's willing to get you there and supervise, it's all right with us," said his mom.

Derek could see that Sharlee was shifting in her chair, itching to get on the phone with her mom and dad. Seizing the moment, he said, "By the way, the kids even said Dave could play too, when he comes!"

"Well, that will be totally up to Dave's parents," said his mom. "We'll get in touch with them, and I'm sure they'll want to speak to your grandma about it too."

While Derek came from a huge extended family, Dave was an only child. His parents were protective, to put it mildly. In fact, they had allowed Dave to sleep over at Derek's only after they'd gotten to know Mr. and Mrs. Jeter personally. Would they let Dave go off now with an aunt or uncle of Derek's, a thousand miles away, to a strange neighborhood for a whole afternoon?

"The last time we talked with them, they said Dave was really looking forward to seeing you," said his mom. "Dave asked if he should bring his golf clubs."

"Umm . . . I don't know," Derek said. "Aren't those kind of heavy?"

"Well, yes," said his dad. "But I think your friend would like to play at least one round while he's over there."

"I guess he can bring them," Derek said. "But tell him not to forget his baseball mitt!"

At that moment Sharlee grabbed the phone out of Derek's hands. "Hi, Mommy! Hi, Daddy!" she said, so excited that she was practically jumping up and down. "Guess what? We're having swimming races tomorrow!"

Derek was about to complain about Sharlee grabbing the phone out of his hands, but he thought better of it. He didn't want to get her upset when she was so happy.

Ten minutes later he managed to get the phone back. "Hi," he said.

"Hi, old man," said his mom. "Your sister sure sounds like she's having a good time. You excited about the swim races too?"

"Oh, I'm not going," he told them. "I'm going to work with Grandpa tomorrow."

"Wow," his dad said, sounding surprised. "That's amazing, Derek. I hope you're up for it."

"No sweat," Derek said. "I've been working so hard all week, my muscles are twice the size they were before."

"Working?" his mom asked.

"Uh-huh. Grandma and I made a deal, that if I worked for the money, Dave and I can go to another Yankees game while he's here."

"And me too!" Sharlee butted in.

"And Sharlee too," Derek repeated into the phone. Sharlee crossed her arms in front of her chest and nodded, satisfied.

"What kind of work?" his dad asked.

"I've been mowing lawns, delivering papers, helping Grandma in the kitchen and with supervising the kids—"

"He's been a good worker!" Grandma called out from the sink, loud enough to be heard over the phone.

"Well, that's just great!" his mom congratulated him. "Good for you!"

"We're proud of you, Son," said his dad.

"I'm just . . . surprised Grandpa agreed to take you," his mom said. "I don't think he's ever taken any of the kids your age to work with him."

"Don't worry, Mom," Derek said. "I can handle it."

"I hope so," said his mom. "In any case, it'll be a great learning experience."

After he hung up with his parents, Derek went back to drying the remaining dishes. He did kind of wish he could stay at the lake with his sister and cousins tomorrow, and be part of the swimming races and contests. But he'd made a commitment to his grandpa, and there was no getting out of it.

"Mmmph." Derek forced one eye open. Grandpa was standing over his bed in the dark, peering down at him.

"It's time," he said softly, so as not to wake Sharlee up. Not that he needed to worry about that. Sharlee always slept like a log.

Derek squeezed his eyes shut and yawned. "What time is it?" he managed to get out.

"Quarter to five. Time to go to work." Grandpa straightened up. "I'll see you downstairs in five minutes. Don't go back to sleep, now."

He left the room, and Derek sat up in bed, knowing that if he didn't, he would indeed go right back to sleep. As it was, he was still half in dreamland, though he couldn't remember what it was he'd been dreaming about.

He stood up, yawned again, stretched, and shuffled off to the bathroom to throw some cold water onto his face and brush his teeth. Then he got dressed and went downstairs, where his grandpa was already eating a bowl of cereal.

"There's yours," he told Derek between mouthfuls, gesturing toward the countertop, where the box of cereal and a gallon of milk stood at the ready. "Don't dawdle, now. We've got to leave in five minutes. Big day ahead."

Derek did as he was told, moving like a zombie, eating silently, just like his grandpa. Who would want to start a conversation at that hour, anyway? It was hard to talk when you were half out of it.

They rinsed off their bowls and went outside. Grandpa led him over to his truck, and they got in. "Buckle up," he told Derek. "This thing's on her last legs. She bounces around some."

Sure enough, the truck must have blown its shock absorbers. Every time Derek started to nod off in the passenger seat, they'd hit a bump and he'd wake back up again. By the time they got to North Arlington, where the church was, it was six a.m. and the sun was rising.

Derek blinked and shielded his eyes from the sun that was peeking out from behind the church, a large white wooden structure with a tall bell tower on the top.

Next to the church itself was a big brick schoolhouse. Derek knew that the church had a school attached to it, but somehow he hadn't realized it was that big a school. It was even bigger than Saint Augustine's in Kalamazoo, where he was a student.

"Well, here we are," Grandpa said, shutting off the engine and putting on his baseball cap. "You ready to get to work?"

"Mm-hmm," Derek mumbled, rubbing the sleep out of his eyes.

"Good. Let's go see what Jordy's up to." Seeing the confusion on Derek's face, Grandpa explained, "Jordy Johnson's my work buddy here at the church. He's a good hard worker. You learn to appreciate that about a person."

"Uh-huh."

"But there is one thing you ought to know about Jordy," Grandpa continued. "He doesn't speak."

Derek cocked his head in confusion.

"Just don't let on that you notice" was all Grandpa said as he got out of the truck.

They found Jordy in the equipment shed, hauling bags of cement off a pile and into a huge wheelbarrow. He was a big, tall man, towering over Derek's grandpa. And Derek could tell by the way he hauled those heavy bags of cement that he was strong, too. "Jordy, this is my grandson Derek. Derek—Jordy Johnson, my partner."

"Pleased to meet you, Mr. Johnson," said Derek. Jordy nodded and smiled at Derek but didn't say anything in return.

"If you need anything out there today," Grandpa told Derek, "just go find Jordy, and he'll help you out."

"Out there?" Derek repeated. "I thought I was going to work with *you*."

"Well, Jordy and I are fixing the sidewalks out front today. That's heavy work. I found something else that needs doing, something you can handle while we're busy with the sidewalks."

He wheeled out a big lawn mower and said, "Since you've got experience at lawn mowing, I figure you'll be able to handle that one job today. Am I right?"

"Just lawn mowing? That's it? Sure thing!" Derek exclaimed, somewhat surprised, and relieved that he wouldn't have to be hauling any sacks of cement. The sacks were nearly his size, and he could clearly read "50 lbs" stamped on the outside of each one.

And mowing only one lawn? Why, he'd mown three in one morning the other day! This was going to be a breeze, he thought.

"Good. Jordy, is she all gassed up?" Grandpa asked, looking at the mower. Jordy nodded, and Grandpa turned to Derek. "Come on, then. You take hold of her and follow me."

Derek pushed the lawn mower out of the shed and followed Grandpa around to the back of the school building, where the athletic fields were.

"Here you go," said Grandpa as they reached the field.

It was already getting hot, and Derek could tell that the day would turn out to be a scorcher. "Empty the clippings in the brush on the sides of the field. There's a water fountain over there if you get thirsty, and a toilet just inside that door."

Grandpa pointed to the nearest door into the school. "Anything else you need, just come and get us. We'll be out front there." With that, he left Derek to his work.

Derek stared out at the football field. He hadn't said anything to Grandpa when he'd first laid eyes on it. But looking at it now, he could see that he had a monster job ahead of him. The field was as big as twenty of the lawns he'd been mowing, and the grass was five times as high! Clearly no one had mowed this field for weeks, probably since the end of the school year.

Derek turned to his task for the day, starting up the big mower and pointing it at the field. *I'm going to show Grandpa I can do this,* he said to himself.

Even though, in his heart of hearts, he was thinking, *No possible way.*

Chapter Ten

CUSTODIANS RULE

The grass was superhigh. The mower weighed a ton and was much harder to push than any he'd worked with before. And the field, to put it mildly, was *huge*.

Derek had to stop every two or three minutes, remove the bag of grass clippings, carry it over to the sidelines, and empty it somewhere in the brush on either side of the field, before reattaching the bag and moving on to the next patch of grass.

By the time he'd gone up and down the field six times, he was already exhausted. He wasn't wearing a watch, but he figured he couldn't have been at it for more than an hour—more like half an hour, probably.

The whole rest of the day, the whole rest of the field,

loomed ahead of him like a giant black cloud. How was he ever going to get through till five o'clock, let alone finish the job his grandpa had given him?

This was *nothing* like the lawns he'd been mowing up till now! Those had been tiny little square patches of sparse grass, with lots of shade from overhanging trees. Here he was totally out in the open, with the sun beating down on him.

By the time the church bells rang eleven, Derek was ready to drop. Instead of carrying the full bag of clippings over to the side of the field, he was dragging the bag. After emptying it, he found himself resting for longer and longer spells there in the shade of the trees, before trudging back into the hot sun and continuing his labors.

He'd been at it for four hours and change now, and the field was not even half done. Even if he kept up this pace all afternoon, he'd be done only just in time for the end of the workday.

Derek had started out with full energy, and now it felt like that energy was almost spent. While he could gas up the mower if it ran out, there was no gassing up the kid pushing it.

Was he imagining it, Derek wondered. Or was it hotter today than it had been all summer? He'd taken numerous breaks for water from the fountain, but he still felt as thirsty as if he hadn't had a drop to drink.

Just as he was about to admit defeat and go tell Grandpa

he couldn't do any more work that day, he felt a big hand gently tapping him on the shoulder.

Derek wheeled around, expecting to see Grandpa but instead saw the kind, smiling face of Jordy Johnson.

"Oh. Hi," Derek said, wiping his brow with his forearm. "How are you?"

Jordy didn't answer, of course. He held up a finger, indicating that Derek should wait a moment. Then he bent down, unhooked the bag of grass clippings, hoisted it onto his shoulder, and headed to the side of the field to empty it.

Derek watched him go, leaning on the mower to rest a little. Jordy had obviously seen him struggling with his job and had come to help.

Looking around, Derek didn't see his grandpa anywhere. Probably he was still working on the cement job out front. Derek wondered if Grandpa had seen Jordy go out to the field, or if Grandpa had actually told Jordy to go check on Derek.

Jordy returned and hooked the bag back up. Then he nodded at Derek and indicated that he should start the mower up again. From then on, every time the bag filled up, Jordy was the one who emptied it.

And fifteen minutes later, when Derek's strength was again nearly at an end, Jordy took over the mowing, too, giving Derek a chance to rest before taking charge of things again.

Soon, thankfully, it was time for lunch. The big sand-wiches Grandma had made them, along with the thermos of iced tea, went a long way toward restoring Derek's strength.

Grandpa asked how it was going, and Derek said, "Fine." But otherwise neither of them talked at all. Derek, for his part, was much too tired to waste energy flapping his lips. *No wonder Grandpa never says much,* he thought.

The afternoon started off with new momentum, but by three thirty Derek was played out again, even worse than before lunch. And once again, with the same perfect sense of timing, Jordy appeared and took the mower from him, giving Derek a chance to rest.

Jordy was a big man, for sure. You could tell he worked hard every day too, because every ounce of him was muscle. Mowing the football field seemed to pose no problem. He gave the mower back to Derek after twenty minutes or so, just long enough for Derek to rest his sore muscles and his hands, which were growing blisters at the base of every finger.

Derek could see the light at the end of the tunnel now. By four forty-five he had only one row left to mow, and he finished it just as the bell at the top of the steeple struck five.

Jordy signaled for Derek to hand over the mower, and he disappeared with the big machine, heading back toward the equipment shed.

Derek went around the front of the church to find his grandpa gathering his supplies and cleaning up. The sidewalk had been repaired, and there were stakes with ropes to keep people off the wet cement till it dried.

"You done with the field?" his grandpa asked.

"Yup!" Derek said, not without a bit of pride, even though he knew he couldn't have done it without help.

His grandpa shook his head. "Took you long enough. I'll bet the grass has grown back by now and needs mowing again."

It was a good thing Derek knew he was joking. That was just Grandpa's sense of humor.

By five thirty everything was put away and it was time to go home. Derek went over to say good-bye to Jordy. "Thanks for the help, Mr. Johnson," he said, shaking Jordy's hand. "I really appreciate it. I couldn't have finished without you."

Jordy waved him off, as if to say, *It was nothing.*

But Derek knew it wasn't nothing. Not at all. Jordy had saved his day and made it a success.

In the truck on the way home, Grandpa, as usual, didn't say much. But what he did say was something Derek would always remember.

"I was glad to see you shake Jordy's hand and call him 'Mr. Johnson,'" he began. "You know, a lot of the kids at the school don't treat him right at all. Make fun of him. Give him no respect. It's not right. Jordy's a good, good man. Those kids could learn a lot about life from him if they'd only pay attention."

After what had happened today, Derek knew it was true. You just never knew who had something to teach you in life, unless you gave them a chance.

"So," his grandpa went on, "now you know what your grandpa does every day for work. What do you think? Would you like to grow up and have my job someday?"

Derek thought about how to answer. He didn't want to hurt Grandpa's feelings. He knew Grandpa did an honest day's work for an honest day's pay—and Derek respected how hard the work was too.

But there was no way he wanted to work that hard every day when he got to be a grown-up. Besides, he already knew what he wanted to do—play shortstop for the Yankees!

"Um . . . ," Derek began.

"That's what I thought," said Grandpa. "Well, there y'go. You know, kiddo, if you want to play professional ball, you have to work harder than everyone else. At everything. You have to practice harder than everyone else."

Derek knew how incredibly lucky he was, to have two parents who were great role models and would do anything to help him achieve his goals, including working two jobs all summer while he went off and had fun.

And his good fortune didn't stop there. He had a grandma who worked all day taking care of the whole extended family, while still finding time to play with him and Sharlee whenever they wanted, and a grandpa who worked his tail off every day to support his family.

They were all great role models, he thought. But they weren't the only ones. Derek had lots of people he looked up to in life. There was Dave Winfield, his favorite baseball player. There was Jumbo over in the Bronx, who played shortstop the way Derek hoped to play the position, and Tiny, who was kind to the other kids and was a good leader, even if he was tough on the outside.

And there was Jordy Johnson, too, who had shown him something today he hadn't realized before: how much a little consideration, a little kindness and helpfulness, can mean to others.

Thanks to Jordy's help, Derek had made a success of his biggest work challenge yet, and had kept his hopes alive of going to that Yankees game with Dave. And before today he hadn't even known Jordy!

Chapter Eleven
CROSSING THE LINE

"Well! There you are!" said Grandma as Derek came down the stairs, rubbing the sleep out of his eyes and yawning. "Do you have any idea what time it is?"

He looked over at the wall clock. "Ten thirty!" he gasped. "Whoa."

"I guess you were tired out after yesterday," she said with a sympathetic smile. "Have a seat. I've got eggs ready for you, if you're ready for them."

Derek nodded, saving himself the effort of opening his mouth and speaking. He was so dog-tired that he could barely move. Every muscle was sore, and he had blisters on his palms from pushing the mower, not to mention the ones on the balls of his feet.

He hobbled over to the table like an old man, and collapsed into a wooden chair. "Ooohhh," he groaned. "Everything hurts."

"Well, I've got something that'll make you feel better," she told him as she brought him a plateful of eggs with a side of home fries and bacon. "Your grandpa said he was proud of you, by the way."

"Really?"

"He told me you mowed the whole athletic field," said Grandma, sitting down opposite Derek and picking up her half-full cup of coffee. "I've been there and seen that field. It's enormous."

Derek let out a laugh, even though it was definitely not funny.

"You've worked very hard, Derek," she went on. "You've earned more than half the money you needed to. And since Grandpa and I want to let you enjoy your free time here too, we've decided to kick in the rest, including a little extra for snacks at the ballpark."

"You mean I get to take Dave to the Yankees game?" Derek could hardly believe it!

"That's right," she said. "We're very proud of you."

"Yahoo!" Derek yelled, springing up from his seat in sheer excitement. "Ow! Ow, ow, ow." He sat back down, slowly and gingerly. Excitement or not, he was going to have to take it easy for a couple of days. Every muscle in his body ached.

But what did it matter? He and Dave were going to see the Yankees! "Awesome!" he said. "Thanks, Grandma! You and Grandpa are the best."

"Well, we know *that*," she said with a little grin.

"I'd get up and hug you, but—"

"I know, I know. I feel old sometimes myself, believe it or not. Oh, and here's another piece of good news. While you and Grandpa were at work, I got a call from your friend Dave's parents. It took a bit of convincing, but they agreed to let him play ball with you in the Bronx, provided I personally am there to supervise."

"Awesome!" Derek shouted, springing up, then wincing in pain as the muscles in his back told him to sit back down.

Then he thought of something else—something really, really important. "Grandma? Do you think we can go see the Yankees on a Wednesday, so we can do both on the same day?"

"Oh! Well, let me see, now. . . . I'll first have to check whether the Yanks are playing at home that day. But it *would* be a lot of fun to see you play. I'd like to see you show off all those new skills of yours in a real, live game. Aunt Dorien and Uncle Ernie tell me those kids are very good players. It sounds exciting!"

Derek could barely contain his happiness. Of course, he already knew the Yankees would be in town the week Dave was coming. He'd made sure of that before he'd even come east for the summer!

Derek was so stoked that he didn't even mind the aches and pains he was feeling. He'd done it! He'd made good on his promise to take Dave to see the Yankees.

And he and Dave were going to get to play ball together with his new friends from the Bronx!

Best of all, Derek had made his grandpa proud, although it had taken Jordy Johnson's help. All in all, working harder than he ever had in his life had been well worth it!

The following Wednesday, two days before Dave was scheduled to arrive, Derek returned to the Bronx with Aunt Dorien. His body had recovered from his monster day of work with Grandpa, and he was eager to get out onto the field, especially since today he'd have the chance to play shortstop.

After hopping out of the car, he jogged over to the kids, who were already busy choosing sides for today's game. Meanwhile, Aunt Dorien parked half a block down. The Yanks were out of town this week, so there was no problem finding parking spaces nearby, and no need to pay for a spot in a crowded parking lot.

"Yo, yo, yo!" called Yo-yo, seeing Derek first. "Jersey Boy is here!"

Funny, being called that, Derek thought. He was much more of a Michigan boy in his own mind, even though he'd been born in New Jersey and spent most of his summers there.

Everyone greeted him with pats on the back or taps of their mitts. Then Jumbo said, "Listen up. I told Derek he could play short today, so we've gotta be on opposite sides, whatever else happens."

Nobody argued with Jumbo, Derek noticed.

Tiny was the other captain, and he motioned Derek over. "Okay, I've got Derek," he said. "Your pick, Jumbo."

"I've got Bluebelly."

"Okay. I've got Pokey."

"I've got Yo-yo."

On and on it went.

The game started with Derek's team at bat. Tiny had him hitting second, right after Pokey—who, like the others, had obviously been given that nickname as a joke. With his lightning speed, he beat out the throw to first after his weak grounder, sending Derek to the plate with a man on.

"Hit a home run, Derek!" he heard his aunt cheer as he stepped into the batter's box. The only other spectators were kids from around the neighborhood, who were as likely to boo as they were to cheer.

The pitcher was a kid they called Doogie, a big kid who looked fourteen, even though Tiny had told Derek he was only twelve. It didn't matter. Doogie could really fire the ball in there.

Derek didn't know if Doogie had a curve or a changeup in his arsenal, but Derek was determined to look for a fastball and try to get out in front of it.

It was difficult because Doogie threw so hard. The first two pitches blew by Derek before he got his bat around. With an 0–2 count and the ball coming in at that speed, Derek could only swing and hope the ball would run into his bat.

CRACK! To his surprise, he hit it! Unfortunately, it was right at Jumbo, who dove to his right and stretched full-out to make the catch in midair. Then Jumbo sprang to his feet and fired to first to double off Pokey, who had sped off for second, sure that the ball was a base hit.

Jumbo shouted in triumph, and the kids who were crowded outside the chain-link fence watching the game whooped it up.

Derek felt bad, but as he returned to the dugout, Tiny said, "Good contact, Jersey. Not your fault. Next time just don't hit it to short."

Jersey. Derek kind of liked it. It was better than Jersey Boy, anyhow. *Jersey Jeter.* Yeah . . . it had a kind of ring to it.

The third out was registered on a strikeout, and Derek's team took the field. Derek threw the ball around the infield with his teammates for a few seconds, and then Jumbo yelled, "Come on, let's go! Play ball!"

Jumbo, as captain, had himself leading off and was already standing in the batter's box, waggling his bat back and forth over his shoulder.

Tiny said, "Easy, easy, man," put on his catcher's mask, and squatted down behind the plate.

Derek bounced lightly up and down on the balls of his feet, in position to catch anything that came his way. He could see Jumbo surveying the field, looking for weak spots where he could hit the ball.

Maybe it was just where the pitch was thrown, or maybe Jumbo did it on purpose because he doubted Derek's abilities at short. Either way, the ball screamed off Jumbo's bat right at Derek, and about four feet over his head. Derek reacted without thinking, darting back, then launching himself at the ball, which was already behind him.

His arm just about left its socket, but he somehow snagged the ball and came down with it in his mitt! He heard a roar go up from the other kids as he threw it back in to the pitcher.

Glancing over at the first-base line, Derek saw Jumbo slam his batting helmet into the ground, so hard that it bounced up and nearly hit him in the face. He looked over at Derek, and there was an expression on his face that Derek had never seen before. What was it? Surprise? Respect? Envy, even?

Derek soon made two more amazing plays at short. The first was a behind-the-back flip to the second baseman, just in time to nip the runner sliding into the bag. On the very next pitch the batter looped a pop fly into short left field. Derek tracked it over his shoulder and made a basket catch to end the third inning!

He noticed that Jumbo kept glancing over at him.

Something was on Jumbo's mind, something to do with Derek. But what was it?

In the fourth, Derek led off the inning. This time he was determined to try to hit it the other way, away from Jumbo at shortstop. In fact, when the pitcher was throwing this hard, hitting to the opposite field was easier than trying to pull the ball. All Derek had to do was slap the ball toward the hole between the first and second basemen.

He let two pitches go by, for a ball and a strike. Then, seeing his pitch coming, he just stuck his bat out to meet it. The ball skittered toward right field. Both the first and second basemen dived for the ball, but neither could come up with it.

Derek was safe at first, but he had no intention of staying there. He took only a small lead on the next pitch, but just as the catcher was about to throw the ball back to the pitcher, Derek took off for second base.

He would have been dead meat if the catcher had still been holding the ball. But the ball had already left the catcher's hand, and by the time the pitcher grabbed it, wheeled around, and threw to second, Derek was already sliding in safely.

"Way to go, Jersey!" Tiny yelled. "We've got us a winner here!" He pumped his fist, then pointed out at Derek. Derek nodded back, trying to be cool, even though he was practically floating on air.

Now it was Tiny's turn to hit. Doogie, the pitcher, tried

to make him swing at bad pitches. Clearly, with first base open, he didn't want to give up a big hit to the other team's best hitter.

But Tiny wasn't up there to walk and leave it up to the next guy. That wasn't the kind of player he was. Derek watched as Tiny reached way out past the plate and managed to get decent wood on a pitch that wasn't more than three inches off the ground. The ball rose into the air, over the first baseman's head, and fell just fair before bouncing into foul territory.

Derek had a good look at the ball off the bat and saw that it was going to fall between the first baseman and the right fielder, who had been playing deep for Tiny. Derek took off at full speed and never stopped until he slid into home with the first run of the game!

"Attaboy, Derek!" he heard Uncle Ernie yelling. "Way to go!"

The score stayed 1–0 into the sixth inning. Jumbo's team was up for their last licks, and Jumbo, who would be fourth to bat in the inning, was clearly itching for a chance to turn the game around.

But first someone had to get on base. And Iceman, who had come on to pitch for Derek's team in the fifth, was dealing. He struck out the first two men, and Derek smelled victory in the air. If they could just get this last guy out, Jumbo would never get to the plate. The game would end with him in the on-deck circle, powerless to change the outcome.

Pokey was a hard kid to strike out because he was so short that his strike zone was tiny. He crouched down in his stance so low that a pitcher had to thread a needle to get a strike on him.

The last thing Iceman wanted to do was walk someone ahead of Jumbo. Behind 3–0, Iceman threw a nice, fat pitch over the heart of the plate, and Pokey whipped a hard grounder back up the middle for a single.

Jumbo clapped his hands and yelled, "Yeah! That's what I'm talkin' about!" Then he spit on his hands, rubbed them together, grabbed his bat, and stepped up to the plate.

Even with that batting helmet on Jumbo's head, Derek could tell that Jumbo was staring out at shortstop. *He wants to hit it to me,* Derek realized. *But why?*

Jumbo already knew Derek could make a play. What was he trying to prove? That even if Derek was good, he, Jumbo, was better?

Derek didn't mind Jumbo's being a better player. To Derek it didn't matter. If someone was better than he was at something, he'd try to learn that person's "tricks," or skills. He'd practice and practice certain details until he felt he had them down and could be confident of them in actual play. And someday, he felt sure, all that work would pay off.

He'd been practicing Jumbo's leap, spin, and throw move all week—whenever his body wasn't in pain, that is. Now, with the game on the line, if Jumbo wanted to hit it to him, Derek thought, *Let him. I'm ready.*

Jumbo had a great eye at the plate. Derek hadn't seen him swing and miss at a pitch all game. When he wanted to hit the ball, he did. For that alone, Derek held him in awe. But Derek wasn't so sure he liked this new side of Jumbo he was seeing. The one where it got *personal*.

With a count of 2–0 Jumbo coiled around like a spring, and let loose on the next pitch, a fastball down at the knees. He smacked it right back up the middle, just a little to the right of the pitcher, who flinched in terror.

Derek sped to his left, behind second base, and grabbed the ball in his outstretched mitt—then pivoted and, falling backward, flicked a sidearm throw to second base. The runner slid, but he was too late. He was out, and the ball game was over!

Derek allowed himself to be mobbed by his new teammates.

"You coming back next week?" one of them asked him.

"Yeah. With my friend Dave," Derek replied.

"All right! Man, you can play some shortstop!"

"Look out, Jumbo," said another. "This kid's gonna put you on the bench! Ha!"

Derek looked around, and there was Jumbo, standing right behind him.

"Over here, Jersey," said Jumbo, beckoning Derek over toward the third-base line, where his team had sat during the game. "I've got something to show you, man."

Derek followed him, although he knew his uncle was

probably waiting for him. He wondered what Jumbo wanted him for. At the fence Jumbo picked up a backpack and fished for something in it. "Yeah, I've got it. Come on back over here for a minute."

He led Derek over to a small concrete shed in foul territory on the left field side. "Around this way," said Jumbo, taking Derek around the back of the little building. "Here you go."

Derek looked at what Jumbo had fished out of his backpack. It was a can of black spray paint. "It's all yours, man," said Jumbo, holding out the can for Derek to take. "You made the grade, Jersey. You're one of us now. Go on and put your tag up there with the rest of them."

Derek looked at the back wall of the shed. It was covered in graffiti!

He could feel his heart pounding underneath his ribs, hear the blood rushing in his ears, hear his breath as loud as thunder.

Graffiti was vandalism, Derek knew. Jumbo was asking him to do something that wasn't just wrong, but was also against the law!

But Derek was afraid to come right out and say that. He was afraid to refuse, too. What if these kids decided not to invite him or Dave back to play ball with them ever again?

Just moments ago he'd been full of the thrill that had come with playing well at a better, higher level. But now Derek wished he could just disappear.

Why, why hadn't he run back to meet Uncle Ernie as soon as the game was over? Why had he even followed Jumbo back here?

"I . . . um . . . have to go. My uncle is waiting back there."

"Aw, man," Jumbo complained, clearly annoyed.

"Really. I have to, right away. Sorry."

"Well, next time, then, for sure," Jumbo said, backing off for now. "I'm not lettin' you off the hook, Jersey Boy."

Derek nodded but didn't say anything. He backed up a few steps, then turned and ran off the field and onto the street, where Uncle Ernie was standing by the benches.

"There you are!" he said to Derek, wearing a big grin. "You were fantastic today, kiddo! When did you get that good?"

"Thanks, Uncle Ernie," Derek said, and gave him a big hug, squeezing tightly. "Thanks."

"Huh? What'd I do?" asked Ernie, puzzled. "Well, never mind. Hugs are always welcome by me."

Derek wished he could tell Uncle Ernie what had just happened. Maybe he would, on the way home. Derek didn't like keeping secrets.

On the other hand, if he told Uncle Ernie, or Grandma, or any of the other adults in his life about what had just happened with Jumbo, they might not let him come back to the Bronx to play with those kids again.

He didn't want to lose that chance, especially not when Dave was coming and would get to be a part of it next week when they went to see the Yankees.

All the way home he thought about what to do. But he didn't say anything. He just sat there, feeling guilty, even though he hadn't really done anything wrong.

Or had he? For sure, he hadn't actually done the deed. But he hadn't come clean about it either. And somehow he felt as guilty about that as if he'd actually sprayed his initials on that concrete wall.

Chapter Twelve
FRIENDS TO THE RESCUE

"Whoo-eee!" Sharlee yelled as she slid down the new slide and cannonballed into the lake. Uncle Jake had put the slide in just before Derek and Sharlee arrived, and it was every kid's new favorite thing. It shot you into the air about three feet above the water, giving you enough time to scream and yell before splashing into the lake.

Derek had been at it as well. His babysitting chores were over now, so he could just join in and let loose like the rest of the kids. But during the time when he'd been working to earn money for the Yankees tickets, he'd become used to watching out for the little ones. Now he still found himself making sure they stayed off the slide, which was for kids five years old and up.

It was past lunch already—midafternoon, the heat of the day. This was the perfect family activity for lazy, hazy days, and all the kids were having a great time, including him.

Except for one little thing. One *eensy, teensy* little nagging thing. He still hadn't mentioned the graffiti incident to Grandma. Nor had he told anyone else. And even though he hadn't done anything wrong, really, he felt more and more burdened by the secret he was keeping.

He'd had a few chances already to come clean to Grandma, and had nearly told her a couple of times, but each time, he'd backed off at the last minute, unsure just how to put it.

He told himself he would find a way to tell her long before next week's game. But every time he didn't say anything, it got harder the next time.

If he hadn't done anything wrong, then why was it proving so hard to talk about it? That was the question he kept asking himself.

The worst part was, Derek knew that next Wednesday, with Dave coming along, he would have to face Jumbo and that spray can again. And this time he wouldn't have a ready excuse.

If Derek agreed to do it, Dave would surely find out and be totally shocked. Even worse, it would be a breach of Derek's contract with his mom and dad, and most of all, it would be just plain wrong.

But if he turned Jumbo down, Derek would risk being called a wimp. It was one thing to have a nickname, but it was another thing if your nickname was "Chicken." Right now those kids thought he was pretty cool. But they wouldn't if Jumbo decided that Derek didn't fit in after all.

"Wheeee!" cried his cousin Jessica, flying off the slide and making a huge splash. Derek smiled and laughed along with the rest of his cousins, but his heart wasn't in it, and his mind was on other things.

He left the lake with Sharlee and Grandma at five and drove back to Grandma and Grandpa's house to shower and get ready for dinner. Tomorrow, thought Derek, Dave would finally arrive. Now, that was something to get excited about!

They'd start out by taking Dave to the lake, where he would meet the whole family and get into some games with the cousins. The second day maybe they'd play that round of golf Dave was dreaming of, or at least go to the driving range. For that he'd have to get Grandma to drive them.

And of course Derek couldn't wait to throw the baseball around with Dave. Maybe his cousin Zach and a few of the older kids would join them, and then the kids could meet up at the local athletic fields sometime when the fields weren't being used. That way Derek could get the chance to try mastering some of those moves he'd seen Jumbo make.

The thought of Jumbo brought Derek back again to the horrible, nagging guilt he'd been feeling. But still he found himself unable to tell Grandma about it. He was just too afraid of how she might react.

As they pulled into the driveway, Derek saw the mailman's truck drive off. "I'll get off here," he told his grandma. She came to a stop, and he got out and grabbed the mail. The car rolled on while he walked slowly up the driveway, examining the day's mail.

A letter for him! From Vijay! Derek broke into a run, stepped inside the house, laid the rest of the mail down on the living room coffee table, took off his sneakers, and sat down to read his good friend's letter—all the way from India!

Derek admired the colorful stamps on the envelope, which was made of very lightweight paper. He tore it open, unfolded Vijay's letter, and read:

Dear Derek,

You can't believe how hot it is here! The monsoon rains are late, and everyone is waiting for them. They are pouring rains, but everybody is happy to see them because we can cool off. That will be good.

The wedding is next week, and already we have had many pre-wedding parties. The dancing goes on and on. I have some new moves to bust out when I come back! I will teach them to you, and maybe we can do them in the Saint Augustine's talent show in October. What do you think? Just like Bollywood movies!

Derek thought of himself as a pretty good dancer, but he'd never been in any kind of talent show and wasn't sure about trying some totally new Bollywood moves in front of his schoolmates.

But you never knew. Vijay sometimes came up with weird ideas that wound up being really good. Maybe there was something there.

The wedding ceremony and feast has seven different parts. But that is not until next week. This week we have the pre-wedding parties. First comes the Haldi ceremony. They cover the bride and groom all over with this sticky paste.

"Eeeuw!" Derek said, making a face.

You may think it's gross, but it's really not, even though it is a bit strange. It's all made from natural things, and it smells like perfume.

For Haldi they put up a canopy of flowers in all colors. Next is the Mehndi ceremony, where the bride and all the young women in the family get their hands and feet painted with henna. It's like a temporary tattoo, and they all go crazy for it. That will be the day before the wedding.

Wait, there's more. Next comes Baraat, when the groom arrives on horseback with his friends and close family. Everyone sings and dances to welcome them. My cousins are trying to teach me the songs, but they're in Hindi, so it's hard for me because I don't remember that much of the language. I was only four when we left here, so . . .

That night comes Milni, where our family will greet the groom's family. We will put flowers around their necks to honor them.

Then we will honor the elephant-headed god Ganesh, for good luck. This is called Ganesh Puja. And all this is before the real wedding! Can you imagine? Now you know why we are away from home the whole summer long! But don't worry, I am having lots of fun.

All my cousins here follow me around all the time, because of my "strange accent" and my American ways. They think I am the coolest, and call me the "American cousin."

Derek paused for a moment. He wished Vijay were there in New Jersey right now, so that Derek could ask him what to do in his own current predicament. Vijay would know what to do, what to say. He always did, somehow.

I will have lots of pictures to show you when I come home. I hope you and Dave are having a good time there in New Jersey. See you in August.

Your friend, Vijay Patel

Derek folded up the letter and put it into his pocket. *Funny,* he thought. *Vijay and I are on opposite sides of the world, but we're both surrounded by cousins who look up to us.*

Well, he could understand why Vijay's cousins would flock around him and look up to him. But his own cousins?

Was he being a good role model to them? How did keeping secrets from the grown-ups in your life fit into that picture?

And tomorrow Dave would be arriving, which would only make telling the truth harder.

"Wow! Are these all *your* suitcases?" Derek was staring at Dave's two big pieces of luggage, and one huge, heavy duffel bag. "All for one week?"

"Well," said Dave with a sheepish grin. "Those are my golf clubs, actually."

"You've got enough here for two months!" Derek said with a laugh. "Well, come on!"

He grabbed one huge suitcase and hoisted the clubs over his other shoulder. "Urghf!" he grunted as he lifted them both off the ground.

Dave grabbed the bigger of the two suitcases, and they slowly made their way out of the terminal and across the street to the parking lot.

"How was your flight, Dave?" Derek's grandma asked him.

"Good," Dave said, beaming. "I can't believe I'm really here, and that my folks actually let me come!"

"Man, I can't wait to get you down to the lake!" Derek said, throwing an arm around Dave's shoulders. "Everyone's waiting to meet you. I talked you up, so don't make a liar out of me, okay? And guess what? I scored us Yankees tickets for next Wednesday night!"

"No way!"

"Yes way!"

"All right!" Dave exulted, high-fiving Derek. "And I looked up golf courses. There's a really good one right near Greenwood Lake we can try out."

"Cool! Um, you brought your mitt, right?"

"Yeah," Dave said. "I knew you'd want me to."

Derek didn't mention his other big surprise—that he and Dave were invited to play ball in the Bronx—for one very good reason. If he did decide to come clean and tell his grandma what had gone down there last time, he risked disappointing Dave if she didn't let them play.

"Wow! This is so awesome!"

Dave was blown away by the Castle, and the lake, and the huge number of kids running around everywhere, playing games, swimming, and laughing up a storm. "This is so different from anything I've ever known. . . ." He fell silent, taking in the chaotic, happy scene.

Derek understood where his friend was coming from.

At home Dave was the only child in a huge house on a huge property, far from other houses, or other kids. Being here, surrounded by at least twenty kids, along with assorted parents, aunts, uncles, and grandparents, was something as strange to Dave as an elephant-headed god would have seemed to Derek's cousins here at the lake.

They spent the afternoon sampling all the fun things to do at the Castle. Derek taught Dave all the water games he and his cousins liked to play—from Marco Polo, to water polo, to backflip contests and, of course, going down the new slide.

Then, when they'd all dried off, Derek and Oscar got everyone together for a quick game of Wiffle ball.

"Half hour, boys!" Grandma called to them, waving. Derek knew that meant she had to get home and start cooking dinner.

Derek turned around to find Dave with a long canvas bag in his hand. "What's that?" he asked.

Dave answered by pulling out a golf club and then shaking out half a dozen Wiffle golf balls! "It's a five iron," he answered. "Anybody want to try hitting a few?"

All the cousins gathered around, eager to try. Golf was one thing that hadn't been a part of their lakeside fun up until that point. But by the time Derek and Dave and Sharlee had to go home with Grandma, everyone was crazy for golf!

Derek felt deeply, truly happy. Not only had New Jersey

and his family made a great impression on Dave, but *Dave* had also made a great impression on *them*.

Tomorrow they'd look into playing some golf. And Derek would make sure they also practiced their baseball fielding, so that he could work on some of those acrobatic moves.

He couldn't wait to take Dave to the Bronx and introduce him to Tiny and the guys, and see the Yankees play the Royals at Yankee Stadium!

And that teeny, tiny little problem? For the moment Derek just forced it out of his mind, telling himself it would work itself out in the end. Hey, maybe Jumbo would forget to bring his spray can, or give up trying to get Derek to do anything dicey.

It was only late that night, after Grandma had said good night, shut off the light, and closed the bedroom door, that the dark thoughts and fears came back to haunt him as he lay in bed.

Earlier that evening Derek's parents had called to see how Dave was doing. And then *Dave's* parents had called to speak to their son, for the very same reason. Obviously both sets of parents were anxious for this visit to work out well, and Derek was happy to be able to report that their first day together had been a smashing success.

But he still hadn't mentioned his dilemma with Jumbo to anyone. Not to his parents, not to Uncle Ernie, not to

Grandma. He didn't even feel like he could tell Dave. He was doomed whatever he did.

What was he going to do? What *should* he do?

He knew what his parents would say.

And that gave him his answer, at long last.

Chapter Thirteen
COMING CLEAN

"Grandma?"

"Derek! I thought you and your friend would sleep in this morning. You were up so late last night."

Derek glanced up at the wall clock that showed it was seven in the morning. "Dave's still sleeping. So's Sharlee, of course."

"Did you come down to get an early breakfast?"

"Um, not exactly. I'm not hungry yet."

"Oh. I see. Then . . . ?"

"I wanted to talk to you about something. Before I talk to Dave about it."

She rinsed off her hands and dried them, then sat him down at the table and took a chair next to him. "All right. What's on your mind this morning?"

"Something that happened the other day," he said, looking at his hands like there was something on them that he needed to examine. "It was while I was playing ball with the kids in the Bronx. . . ."

"Yes?"

"One of them wanted me to . . . to do something that . . ."

"Something you didn't want to do?"

Derek nodded. "And I didn't do it either. But . . ."

"But it took you until now to tell me about it."

"Uh-huh." Derek bit his lip. "I thought if I said anything, you might not let Dave and me play there next week."

"What was it that this boy wanted you to do?"

Derek told her, then watched for her reaction. Grandma nodded slowly, staring into space, as if she were imagining the scene. Then she shook her head. "I'm sorry that happened to you, Derek—and I'm very glad you said no."

Derek hadn't exactly come right out and said no. but he hadn't done the deed either. So he didn't interrupt her.

"What concerns me most," she continued, "is that you didn't come to me right away. Grandpa and I are in charge of your care, and so was Uncle Ernie that day. You could have told him, too. In fact, you should have."

"I know, Grandma. I'm sorry. I just . . ."

"You just didn't want to have to stop playing with those boys," she finished for him. "I understand." She heaved a big sigh. "Derek, if I trust you to go off and mingle with boys we're not well-acquainted with, it's only because you're a good boy and you usually make good decisions. But if you want the grown-ups who are responsible for you to keep on trusting you, you're going to have to trust *them* enough to be honest, and not keep things secret— *especially* uncomfortable things."

Derek nodded. "I know, Grandma. I should have told someone. I will from now on, I promise."

"Hmm. All right, then. I suppose I can let it go, just this once. Especially since you did come and tell me about it in the end. Besides, next week I'll be there myself to keep an eye on things."

"Thanks, Grandma!" Derek said, getting up and throwing his arms around her. "Thank you soooo much!"

"Now, calm down!" she said, peeling his arms off her shoulders. "I will expect you to be watching out for your friend, making sure he's having fun. I'm sure a lot of those boys are perfectly nice, but it only takes one bad apple . . ."

Derek thought about Jumbo. Certainly he was a great shortstop, and Derek wanted to imitate his play out in the field. But Jumbo hadn't been a very good role model when he'd tried to get Derek to do graffiti, had he?

"You know, Derek, as you get older, you'll find yourself in other situations like this. The important thing you have to remember is to always do the right thing, no matter how much peer pressure you're under or how much you want to hang out with certain people."

"Don't worry. I will, Grandma. And I'll look out for Dave, too," Derek promised.

"Good. Then I think we can go ahead with our plans for next week. But you know, you won't always have someone there on the spot watching over you. In the end the courage to do the right thing has to come from *you*."

"Sure, Grandma. I understand—and I promise."

He would have promised her the moon at that moment. He was so glad she hadn't called the whole thing off!

But as the week wore on and their day in the Bronx loomed closer, Derek began to feel more and more nervous about how things would actually go down.

He knew that Jumbo would have that spray can waiting for him the minute he and Dave showed up at the field. And if Derek had to run straight to Grandma and report what was happening, those kids would all think he was a tattletale and a baby! They'd call him all kinds of names, right in front of Dave, and they wouldn't let him hang out with them anymore.

"We're almost there!" Derek said excitedly. "This is the George Washington Bridge. See the city over there?"

"Sure do!" Dave said. "But where's Yankee Stadium?"

"That's in the Bronx. A little bit farther."

Derek could hardly believe that it had already been five days since Dave had arrived. They'd been so busy having fun that the time had flown by!

They'd gone to the driving range, played mini-golf, and even nine holes of real golf, not to mention swimming down at the lake every day, and hanging out with Derek's dozens of cousins. They'd seen a movie, had cookouts, gone bowling, and practiced their baseball skills too, because Derek had wanted to make sure they both played well in their game today.

Derek was so excited, he'd forgotten all his worries for the moment. But if *he* wasn't worried, Dave certainly was. "What if I mess up out there?" he asked nervously. "What if I make an error or something? What if I strike out three times and cost our team the game?"

"Come on, Dave," Derek said, making a face. "You're a good ballplayer! I taught you myself, right?" He elbowed his friend playfully. "Besides, you've been coached by my dad and Chase, the best coaches in the world!"

Chase was Dave's family's driver, and he was the one trusted to take care of Dave whenever his parents went away on business, which was often.

"It's going to be fine. *You're* going to be fine," Derek told him.

Derek could understand why Dave was so nervous. All week long Derek had been telling Dave what good players the Bronx kids were. "You're going to want some of their autographs, I'm telling you," he'd said. "Because they're going to be famous someday."

"I can't believe I'm going to get to see the Yankees, live!"

Dave said. "I've never been to any kind of baseball game outside of Little League, let alone to Yankee Stadium!"

"The cathedral of baseball. Once you see it, you'll never forget it," Derek promised.

"I just hope I can get through this game first, without anything bad happening."

"Nothing bad is going to happen. It's going to be fine, I'm telling you!"

But even as he said it, Derek's own fears returned. Jumbo would be waiting, with his spray can of black paint. And what was Derek going to do then?

Chapter Fourteen

THE ULTIMATE TEST

"Yo, yo, yo! Jersey's back, and he's not alone!"

Yo-yo directed everyone's attention to the two boys from Kalamazoo as they entered the sandlot through the gap in the chain-link fence.

"Lookit, they've both got their Yankees gear on," said Pokey. "Man, I'd like to get me one of those!"

"Who's your friend?" T-Bone asked, looking Dave up and down. Derek knew T-Bone was just being curious, but he could also see that Dave was a little nervous because of the attention.

"This is my buddy Dave, " Derek said, putting an arm around Dave's shoulder. He had to reach up to do it, because Dave was about five inches taller.

"Where'd he get all those freckles?" asked Yo-yo. "Or are they the stick-on kind?"

That made everyone laugh—even Dave. A couple of the kids clapped him on the back, as a kind of salute for being a good sport and letting them goof on him.

Dave had passed his first test, Derek was relieved to see. Now all Dave had to do was play his best baseball, and he'd really have made the grade.

Jumbo and Tiny were captains, as usual. Tiny chose Derek first. And then, after Jumbo chose Pokey, Tiny, with a glance at Derek, took a chance and chose Dave. Dave looked relieved to be on Derek's team, and of course Derek could understand why.

As different as these kids were from Derek and most of his friends back home, they weren't *that* different. Dave, though, was different from everybody else Derek knew, even back in Michigan. His family was rich, and his house wasn't near any other houses, so Dave had to be driven everywhere by Chase in the family's Mercedes.

Derek would have bet that if these kids found out Dave was rich and into golf, they'd be teasing him about it from now until forever.

Still, kids were kids, and baseball was the great unifier. Derek had faith that Dave would improve his game for the occasion, and that the two of them would represent Kalamazoo well here in New York City.

"Hey, Jersey." It was Jumbo, coming up behind Derek

and tapping him on the shoulder. Derek turned to him, saw that Jumbo was holding his backpack in his hand, and froze.

"I've got something for you, like I promised."

Derek had a feeling he knew what was in that backpack. But he didn't want to know for sure, because if it was what he thought it was, he'd have to go straight over and tell Grandma. And that would be the end of everything, before the game even got started!

"Uh . . . show me later, okay, Jumbo?" he blurted out in a near panic, before Jumbo could actually reach into the backpack and show him what was inside. "After the game, okay? I've got to keep an eye on my friend."

There. He'd put off his moment of reckoning. Jumbo let out a quick, scornful laugh. "Yeah, right. Sure thing. I'll hit you up after. But don't go running off, Jersey. I'll be looking for you."

Derek got his meaning. Either he hung around after and did what Jumbo was asking him to, or he wouldn't be welcome to join them again.

"Whoa," Dave said as they got ready to start the game. "This sure is different from our league in Kalamazoo. These kids can really be tough on you, can't they?"

"Don't take it the wrong way," Derek advised him. "They mess around that way with each other too all the time. It's their way of having fun. Just go with it, like you were doing, and you'll be fine."

Derek started the game at shortstop, with Dave playing left field behind him. Dave's usual position was third base. But luckily, Derek's dad had insisted the previous season that everyone on the team spend time playing different positions, just to have the experience, in case they needed it down the road.

Hopefully that experience would come in handy today.

Derek got ready, and his team's pitcher, a pudgy kid nicknamed Baby, wound up and fired a fastball for a strike to start the game.

Derek turned around to see Dave out there, pounding his glove and bouncing up and down on the balls of his feet, just like Derek's dad and Chase had taught all their players to do.

On the second pitch the hitter rifled a line drive over Derek's head that curved toward the foul line. Dave got a good jump on it, dived headlong, and grabbed it! He slammed to the ground and slid another three feet in the dirt, kicking up a dust storm.

"Whoo-eee!" Baby yelled, along with the rest of them. "Way to go, Spots!"

"Kid can play!" Tiny shouted, pointing out at Dave from the catcher's position behind home plate.

Spots, huh? Derek thought. Well, considering Dave's freckled face, they could have thought of worse nicknames.

Derek turned around and gave Dave a thumbs-up as Dave got up and dusted off his jeans and Yankees jersey.

Derek knew they were expensive too. Dave's jersey was brand-new, and his jeans were always pricey and in the latest style. But it didn't matter now. Once you covered them with dirt, fancy new clothes looked the same as crummy ones.

Dave shot Derek a big grin in return and pointed with his glove. Clearly he was feeling a lot better now about being a part of this whole new adventure.

Their team got out of the top of the inning without giving up a run. Then, after a leadoff double, Derek found himself at the plate, with a man on second and nobody out.

He swung at the first pitch and fouled it back, right into the catcher's mask. The catcher staggered backward and fell against the backstop, stunned.

Tiny rushed out from the bench and squatted down next to the catcher. Derek too came over to see if the kid was okay.

"You don't look so good," Tiny told the kid. "Go sit down for a while. I'll sub for you."

Derek was puzzled. Tiny was on the opposing team and was a fierce competitor. But in this "league," where the only rules were the ones the kids decided to play by, it was obviously okay to switch teams for a while, in case of an emergency.

The catcher who'd taken the hit protested that he was okay, but Tiny insisted that he sit down for this inning, or at least until it was Tiny's turn to bat. Then Tiny put on the catcher's mask, got his own mitt, put on the shin guards and chest protector, turned to Derek, and told him to get back in the batter's box.

Derek took a couple of pitches. Then, with a count of 1–2, he laced a single to right that scored the runner from second!

On the first pitch to the next hitter, Derek decided to spring a surprise and steal second base. Tiny was startled at first but recovered quickly and fired a laser beam to nail Derek by a hair for the out.

"Oh! What a play! Yes!" cried Jumbo at short, pumping his fist.

"Yo, what'd you do that for?" Yo-yo complained from the bench. "You're supposed to be on our team, Tiny!"

"I'm on their team right now," Tiny shot back. "Whatever team I'm on, I do my best. You got a problem with that?"

Yo-yo didn't answer.

"That's what I thought," said Tiny.

Derek got up and dusted himself off, then pointed in to Tiny and clapped his hands in front of him, saying "Great play!"

Tiny pointed back at him and nodded, and Derek felt they understood each other. Derek couldn't help feeling that he and Tiny thought alike, and that Tiny was the kind of kid he would want to be friends with, no matter where they ran into each other.

The hitter struck out, and now it was Tiny's turn to hit. He took off the catcher's gear, looked over at the kid who'd been hit in the mask, and asked if he was okay to catch. The kid got up off the bench, gave Tiny five, and took the catcher's gear from him.

Now Tiny was back on his own team, and it didn't take long for him to make up for the damage he'd done to them while subbing for the other team. He hit a bomb to center that went way over the fielder's head. Tiny circled the bases and scored easily to make the score 2–0.

The inning ended quietly after that, and soon the momentum swung back the other way.

Jumbo's team kept hitting line drive after line drive off Baby. After they'd tied the game and put another man on base, Tiny made a switch and brought Yo-yo in from second base to pitch.

Yo-yo, it turned out, was a guy who liked to get hitters out with trickery rather than with speed. He threw all kinds of quirky pitches—quick pitches, slow pitches, curving and screwballing ones.

That was fine, as long as there was no one on base. But every time a runner got on, they wound up getting to second and third because Yo-yo's pitches kept getting away from Tiny.

One kid even stole home when a pitch bounced off Tiny and up the first-base line! Soon it was 5–2, Jumbo's team.

But Tiny's guys came back in their half of the fourth, with five big runs, the last two coming on another long home run by Tiny himself.

If Derek thought his team was finally back in charge, he was soon shown otherwise. Jumbo started the rally in the fifth with a triple, and only a good, long throw by Dave to get the ball back in from deep left field kept it from being a home run.

Jumbo scored anyway, though, when, with two outs, another of Yo-yo's trick pitches got away from Tiny.

"Come *on*!" Baby whined from second base, where he'd been playing since Tiny had switched him out. "Put me back in, Tiny! I'm good to go!"

"Hey, that run was on me," Tiny told him. "You just do your own job and let Yo-yo do his."

"Man!" Baby groused, but he stopped complaining after that. And when the next batter shot a screamer his way, he calmly grabbed it for the third out.

"*That's* what I'm talking about!" Tiny told him when they got back to the bench, clapping him on the head with his catcher's mitt.

The score was 7–6 when the sixth inning began, but something told Derek that the game was far from in the bag. Sure enough, with one out, Jumbo singled to right field. The next hitter hit a soft grounder to Baby, who grabbed it and flicked it to second base.

Derek, racing over from short to take the throw, knew it would be a difficult double play to turn. But if he succeeded, the game would be over!

He came to the bag quickly and grabbed the toss—but

just then Jumbo came barreling into him, sending Derek into a somersault and almost causing him to drop the ball!

Jumbo was out, but the batter had made it to first base safely, and that proved to be super-important, because the next batter hit the ball high and far for the go-ahead home run!

Even though Yo-yo came back to strike out the next hitter, Derek's team was still behind, with only three outs left to stage a comeback. But nobody was down in the dumps. In a game like this one, it wasn't over till it was over.

Dave was leading off. He'd already walked and had an infield single, but he hadn't really made good contact with a pitch all day.

Derek had noticed that in the weeks since they'd last played ball, Dave's swing had gotten loopy again, like when he'd first started playing baseball. It was more of a golf swing than a baseball swing, and it had taken Derek a while to help him change it to a more level swing.

Derek wanted to remind Dave about it now, but he didn't want to mess with his friend's confidence in the middle of a game. Dave was already probably feeling anxious, trying to impress the other kids, just like Derek had been during his first game here.

So instead of saying something to Dave about changing his swing, Derek just told him, "Make the pitcher get the ball down. Don't swing at anything above the belt."

Dave looked puzzled, but he'd known Derek long enough, and trusted his baseball smarts enough, to nod his head and say, "Okay." Derek just hoped Dave would get a low pitch to hit with that golf swing of his.

Dave let two high strikes go by. He looked doubtfully at Derek, but Derek just nodded slowly, to show that he still thought Dave should stick to the plan.

The next pitch was a ball outside. The one after that was over Dave's head, and now the count was even at 2–2.

Finally the pitcher threw a fastball down at the knees—right where Dave's swing could get at it. Dave practically jumped out of his shoes, swinging so hard that he nearly fell down. But he made solid contact, and the ball got between the outfielders for a leadoff double! Dave clapped his hands together as he reached second, and pointed in to Derek as if to say, *Thanks.*

The next hitter dribbled one in front of home plate, and the catcher faked a throw to second, forcing Dave back to the bag, before throwing to first for the out.

Now Derek came up to bat. He knew he had to make contact and get the ball out of the infield. Seeing that there was a big hole between the first and second basemen, he slapped the first pitch that way. It skidded between them and into the outfield!

Dave barreled into third, and seeing his teammates windmilling their arms, he kept on going, steaming toward home. The throw came in, but the tag was too late. Tie game! Dave popped up and pounded his hands together, shouting, "YEAH!"

Derek had taken advantage of the throw home to make it to second base. Standing there now he noticed, though Dave seemed to have no idea, that Dave had ripped a hole in the knee of his pants. *Oh, well,* Derek thought with a grin. *They died a hero's death.*

He could only watch now, and hope that one of the next two hitters would drive him in with the winning run. The first man up, though, struck out on three straight blazing fastballs. The next man walked.

Next up was Tiny himself, and Derek was glad it was him. If anybody could deliver a clutch hit off a tough pitcher, it was the captain.

Tiny worked the count to 3–2, then fouled off three straight pitches, two of which would have been ball four.

He doesn't want to walk, Derek realized. *He doesn't want to leave it for the next guy.* He *wants to be the one to drive in the winning run.*

The next pitch wasn't over the plate, but it was close enough for Tiny to get a good swing on it and send it out into right field, just over the first baseman's head.

Derek was off and running, and he never slowed down till he went into his slide. The ball came in to the plate ahead of Derek. The catcher grabbed it and stuck his mitt out to make the tag. But Derek's foot came in so hard, and so fast, that it knocked the ball right out of the catcher's mitt for the winning run.

Game over! 9–8!

Derek popped up and joined his teammates in celebrating, jumping up and down and high-fiving one another.

"Man, that was amazing!" Dave said, with a silly grin spread all over his face. "That was so awesome!"

"You played great!" Derek told him. "You ripped your good pants, though."

Dave looked down, saw the hole in his jeans, and laughed. "Yeah? Well, yours are ripped too, smart guy."

Derek looked down to see that he, too, had a hole in his pants! He must have ripped them sliding into the plate just now.

Not that he cared. They'd played, and won, one of the greatest games of their lives!

What a feeling!

"Hey. Jersey."

Derek's heart sank in a split second.

"Jumbo! Hey."

"It's time. Come on, let's go."

Derek turned to Dave, not knowing exactly how to explain to his friend what was going on. But Dave had disappeared.

Through the crowd of kids chest-bumping and high-fiving, Derek saw Dave talking to Grandma by the benches on the other side of the fence.

Derek turned back to Jumbo. "Uh . . ."

"You coming? Or not?"

"I . . . uh . . ."

"Hey! *Hey!*"

Startled, Derek turned to see Tiny advancing on them, an angry look on his face. "What's going on, Jumbo? What're you trying to pull now?"

"Man, *you* know," Jumbo said. "He's part of our thing now, so I was—"

"Don't even *think* about it." Tiny jabbed a finger at Jumbo. "Don't go draggin' him into any of that stupid stuff you guys do."

"What, you think he's better than us?" Jumbo shot back angrily.

"I don't see *him* acting like a big shot, messing up walls with spray paint. Do you?"

"Come on, man! Lots of kids do like that," Jumbo insisted.

"This place belongs to everybody, not just you. You should show some respect."

Derek was stunned. Hadn't Jumbo suggested that *all* the kids had put their initials on the wall? He'd taken Jumbo's word for it that they had. But now it was clear that Tiny, at least, would never do something like that, and that Jumbo had been lying to Derek.

Tiny turned his attention to Derek. "You know, you don't have to do something just because some clown tells you to. You just do what you think is right. Stick with that."

Derek nodded. "Thanks, Tiny. I *mean* it. I don't do stuff like that. But anyway, thank you, guys, for letting me and Dave play here with you. It's been amazing."

"What? You're not coming back next week?" Tiny asked, surprised. "I thought you said you were here for the whole summer."

"Next time you come," Jumbo said, "I've got a new nickname for you. You want to hear it?"

"Don't listen to this clown," Tiny told Derek. "He's always getting himself and everybody else in trouble. You do what you've got to do—whatever you think is right— and never mind what he calls you."

Derek nodded.

"I hope we see you next week, Jersey," Tiny added, seeming to read Derek's mind. "But either way, it's been good knowing you. Go on now. You've got a Yankees game to catch, right?"

"Right," said Derek, only now remembering that it was almost game time. "Well . . . I hope I *do* see you guys again sometime."

"Yeah," said Jumbo, hanging his head a little in embarrassment.

"Hey, me too," Tiny said, shaking Derek's hand. "Maybe one day we'll see each other over there, huh?" He nodded toward the big ballpark across the street, and smiled. "You never know. You've got some skills, man. Keep working at it."

"Thanks, Tiny!" Derek said. "You guys too. *All* of you. You guys deserve a real league of your own. And I hope you get to have one again soon." With that, he jogged over to where Dave and his grandma were waiting.

"What happened back there?" Dave asked. "What took you so long?"

Derek looked at him, at Sharlee and Grandma, and said, "I'll tell you later."

He would too. Not Sharlee, of course. He wouldn't want to upset her with it. And not right now. Not when they were about to go see the Yankees, Dave's first big-league game ever!

They crossed the street and got in the ticket holders line, and Derek felt his anxieties melting away. He and Dave had just played in—and won—an amazing game, with an incredible bunch of ballplayers.

And now, to top it all off, they were going to see the real Yankees play!

Chapter Fifteen

BASEBALL HEAVEN

From the time they entered the stadium, to the moment when they walked through the passageway and into the upper deck seating area, all Dave kept saying was "Whoa." His eyes were as wide as they could stretch, and his mouth hung open too.

Sharlee was hopping up and down with excitement. "This is my second time this summer!" she told the people they passed on their way to their seats.

"Is that really *Dave Winfield* down there?" Dave finally said, pointing down at number 31 in right field, who was tossing a ball around with the center fielder, warming up.

"That's him, all right!" Derek said. "And there's Rickey Henderson over there, and Don Mattingly."

"I just can't believe how many people are here!" Dave enthused. "I've never seen so many people in one place before."

"There might be forty thousand or so," Grandma told him.

"Wow. It looks more like forty million!" said Dave.

"That's silly," said Sharlee. "Forty million is, like, twice as many as this."

Derek laughed. "Sharlee, did you count that out on your fingers?"

"No, but I *did* count out that cotton candy is three dollars! Are you going to buy me one?"

Everyone laughed. "As a matter of fact," said Derek, "I *did* bring some 'moolah' along with me, just in the unlikely case you wanted something to eat."

"Sandwiches first, sweets second," Grandma said, laying down the law, in spite of the big frown Sharlee put on.

Derek knew his little sister would eat whatever it took to get to the cotton candy. When she wanted something badly enough, she was sure to get it sooner or later. Just like him, with his dream of playing for the Yankees.

Sharlee never quit, and neither would he, until he was down there on that infield—and not just in his dreams!

They ate their sandwiches and settled in to watch the game. The Yankees were playing the Kansas City Royals today, and they all watched as the two teams dueled it out, trading runs, and leads, back and forth.

By the sixth inning, when Sharlee had finished her cotton candy and was working on a chocolate ice cream in a little blue plastic Yankees cap, the score on the field was 8–7, Kansas City.

Dave Winfield was at the plate with two on and two out, two balls and two strikes. "Come on! Hit one out here!" Dave stood up and yelled at the top of his lungs.

Derek grinned. Dave was so into the game that he'd forgotten his usual shyness. It didn't matter here, anyway. Everyone else was screaming their head off too. It was so loud that the stands were literally vibrating!

On the very next pitch Winfield launched a high, arcing fly ball way into the sky. "It's coming this way!" Dave shouted.

It *was* coming their way. Even though they were sitting in the upper deck, Winfield had so much power that he could reach that far. To Derek's utter amazement, it seemed to be coming straight for them!

Derek was already standing, and now he reached up to try to grab the ball. But it was coming so fast and so hard that he felt a little tinge of fear at that instant. Everybody was reaching out for the same home run ball.

At the last moment a big guy in the row behind them lunged forward and managed to flick the ball away from Derek's outstretched hands. The ball fell to the floor—where who should pick it up, being closest to the ground, but Sharlee!

"I *got* it! I *got* it!" she shrieked, holding it up. *"I got it!"*

Derek could not believe it. Of all the people reaching for it, it had been Sharlee who'd ended up with the ball. Why, she hadn't even been watching when Winfield had hit it—and had only looked up when everyone around her had stood up and started yelling.

"Wow, Sharlee! Good for you!" said Grandma. "Great catch!"

"Yaaaaay!" Sharlee said, holding the ball up again for everyone to see. The people in the stands nearby gave her a big round of applause as Winfield rounded the bases, putting the Yankees in the lead, 10–8.

Derek winced and suppressed a groan. He would have had it! If only that guy behind him hadn't reached for a ball he had no chance of catching, it would have been Derek who'd made the catch!

"Do you think we could wait around after the game to get Dave Winfield to sign it?" he asked Grandma.

"I don't think so, Derek. It's been a long game. We're not going to be able to stay after."

"Aww." Derek was disappointed—doubly so because it had been Sharlee, not him, who'd wound up with the ball. After all, Winfield was *his* hero, not hers.

"I'm sorry, hon. Next time you go see the Yanks, bring it with you, and maybe he'll sign it then."

They settled back down, and the game went on. The Royals tied it back up in the top of the ninth, but in the bottom of the inning, Don Mattingly hit a walk-off solo shot to win the game for the Yanks!

"I can't believe how it ended!" Dave was raving as they left the building and headed for the parking lot. "Man, that was unbelievable!"

They kept on reliving the game, and the one they'd played in themselves beforehand, all the way back to Greenwood Lake, where they pulled into the driveway right behind Grandpa's pickup truck as he was returning from work. Then, over a very late dinner, they told Grandpa all about their day in the Bronx. Sharlee showed him the home run ball, which particularly seemed to impress him.

"You caught this, huh?" he asked her as she squirmed in his lap. "Your hands must have been pretty sticky from all that cotton candy. I don't know how else you managed to get it, with all those greedy big people grabbing for it."

"I don't know. I just *did*!" she exulted.

"Watch out for this one," he told Grandma, nodding toward Sharlee. "Nobody's going to get in *her* way!"

That night as they lay in their beds, Derek finally told Dave what had happened after the game back at the sandlot. He'd already told Grandma while they'd been washing dishes before going up to bed. And as Derek had expected, she'd suggested that maybe he'd gone to the city enough for one summer.

Sharlee was sleeping in the guest bedroom for the week, so Derek didn't have to worry about her waking up and overhearing him and Dave talking.

"Wow," Dave said after Derek had told him about Jumbo trying to get Derek to deface the wall of the equipment shed. "I can't believe kids do that stuff."

"They don't *all* do it," Derek corrected him. He told Dave about Tiny telling Jumbo off.

"Gee," Dave said, still shaken. "Things sure are different here in New York."

"Not really," said Derek. "I've heard of this kind of thing happening in Kalamazoo, too."

He remembered that when he'd first seen Jumbo, he'd wanted to be just like him—carry himself in that cool way, and casually make great plays in the field like they were nothing. But when he'd seen Jumbo spitting on the ground, and taking advantage of an injured player, it had changed Derek's view of him. And the graffiti incident had made it obvious that Jumbo was not someone to take after off the field.

Derek had learned a lot about role models lately. He'd always looked to his parents, of course, and his grandma. Vijay, too, in many ways was someone Derek looked up to.

But this summer he'd found some new role models. Starting with his grandpa, whom he'd come to appreciate in a new, deeper way.

Then there was Jordy Johnson. Who would have

thought that he'd have anything important to teach Derek about life? But he *had*.

Finally there was Tiny. Although he didn't have Jumbo's cool factor, and he seemed kind of mean at first glance, he really had turned out to be someone to admire—both on the field, with his toughness, and off the field, with his kindness and his firmness in protecting Derek from being led into a big, big mistake.

"You know what?" Derek said. "When I get older, I want to be a leader—like a team captain or something."

"Like Jumbo and Tiny?" Dave asked.

"Well, not like Jumbo, but yeah. You know, guiding the other kids on the team to be their best all the time, not just on the field."

He thought of his cousins at the lake, especially all the younger ones. He was going to be sure to be a role model for them for the rest of the summer too.

The two friends fell silent. Outside they could hear the tree frogs making a racket. Dave had been a little nervous the first night he'd heard them croaking away in the darkness. But Derek had found one and shown it to him, and after that, Dave had been fascinated by them, not creeped out.

"I wish I didn't have to leave tomorrow," Dave said finally. "This has been an amazing week."

"I know. I told you it would be."

"Maybe next year we can do it again?"

"Yeah, and get Vijay to come too!"

After another brief silence Dave said, "Hey, Derek? Do you remember the first time we met, and you tried to become friends with me?"

"Yeah, I remember. You wouldn't give me the time of day."

"I know. Sorry. I didn't know anybody in town, and here was this kid who wanted to be my friend. . . . Anyway, I just wanted to say you've been my *best* friend, ever—not just a good one."

"Aw, be quiet, now. You're embarrassing me."

"Okay, okay." After another silence Dave said, "Hey, are you going to try out for basketball this fall?"

"I was thinking about it," Derek said. "I'd been thinking maybe I should just concentrate on baseball, but then I remembered that Dave Winfield was drafted in three sports. He could have been a star in any one of them. So maybe, yeah, I might."

"I will if you will," said Dave.

That made Derek sit up in bed. "That *would* be kind of cool," he had to admit.

Dave was really tall for his age, and they had played enough one-on-one games for Derek to know that Dave could play some defense. His jumper needed work, but it would be a blast for both of them to play on Saint Augustine's team this fall.

For Derek, competition was as natural as breathing. It

made him feel totally alive and excited. Besides, no matter how hard he concentrated on baseball, a kid had to have fun during the offseason too, didn't he?

Derek knew he had a long road ahead of him if he wanted to go from playing in Yankee Stadium's shadow to playing in the stadium itself.

But he was sure that if he stayed on the right path, worked hard, and didn't let himself go astray, he had a chance to make it there someday, *especially* if he kept collecting the best role models he could find—from custodians, like Jordy; to friends, like Dave and Vijay; to family, like his parents and grandparents; to kids he would meet along the way, like Tiny.

"We're going to get there someday," Dave said in the darkness, as if he were reading his friend's mind. "You watch."

"We will," Derek agreed. "But you know what? Nobody gets there alone."

JETER'S LEADERS

is a leadership development program created to empower, recognize, and enhance the skills of high school students who:

- ◉ **PROMOTE HEALTHY LIFESTYLES AND ARE FREE OF ALCOHOL AND SUBSTANCE ABUSE**

- ◉ **ACHIEVE ACADEMICALLY**

- ◉ **ARE COMMITTED TO IMPROVING THEIR COMMUNITY THROUGH SOCIAL CHANGE ACTIVITIES**

- ◉ **SERVE AS ROLE MODELS TO YOUNGER STUDENTS AND DELIVER POSITIVE MESSAGES TO THEIR PEERS**

Photo credit: Eileen Barroso/Turn 2 Foundation, Inc.

"Your role models should teach you, inspire you, criticize you, and give you structure. My parents did all of these things with their contracts. They tackled every subject. There was nothing we didn't discuss. I didn't love every aspect of it, but I was mature enough to understand that almost everything they talked about made sense." —DEREK JETER

DO YOU HAVE WHAT IT TAKES TO BECOME A JETER'S LEADER?

- I am drug and alcohol free.
- I volunteer in my community.
- I am good to the environment.
- I am a role model for kids.
- I do not use the word "can't."
- I am a role model for my peers and younger kids.
- I stand up for what's right.

- I am respectful to others.
- I encourage others to participate.
- I am open-minded.
- I set my goals high.
- I do well in school.
- I like to exercise and eat well to keep my body strong.
- I am educated on current events.

CREATE A CONTRACT

What are your goals?

Sit down with your parents or an adult mentor to create your own contract to help you take the first step toward achieving your dreams.

For more information on JETER'S LEADERS, visit
TURN2FOUNDATION.ORG

BULLYING.
BE A LEADER
AND STOP IT.

Turn the page
for a sneak peek at
Fast Break

Chapter One

"It's a rocket to short—OOHH! Jeter makes the diving stab going away from first, then throws from his knees and nails the runner! What a play! That's one for the ages, folks! Let's watch it one more time, in slow motion. . . ."

"Derek! Are you with us?"

Derek Jeter snapped to attention, his beautiful daydream gone in an instant. The whole class full of sixth graders laughed.

"Yes, Ms. Terrapin, I'm listening. Sorry."

"Summer is over, everyone," said the teacher. "I know it's still early September, and it's warm and sunny and beautiful outside—but we've got a lot of work to cover, and I need your attention."

The trouble was, summer *was* over. It felt like a million years since Derek was up at his grandparents' place in Greenwood Lake, New Jersey.

It had been the best summer ever! Derek's best friend Dave Hennum had come for a week to join him. They had played baseball with a bunch of city kids in the Bronx, who would have all been Little League all-stars—if only they'd had a league of their own.

After playing ball with them, Derek's game was better than ever. He couldn't wait to play again! In fact, he'd just gotten caught daydreaming about it.

Too bad his next chance was seven months away. In the meantime, all he could do was play pickup games on Jeter's Hill—the sloping patch of grass in Mount Royal Townhouses, where Derek spent so much of his time that the other kids had named it after him.

In a month or so, cold weather would force everyone else indoors—but not Derek. From October through March, the only kid in Kalamazoo who thought it was warm enough to play baseball was Derek.

He would go to the batting cages with his dad every once in a while, of course, but that was about it. And Derek could feel already that it wouldn't be nearly enough to see him through till spring. No, he was going to have to find something *else* to do until then.

But what?

"Class," said Ms. Terrapin, interrupting his train of

thought, "in a couple of weeks we will be moving forward into the wild worlds of algebra, chemistry, biology, and earth science."

There were murmurings from all around the room. "Ugh. Sounds *hard*," Derek heard Sam Rockman mutter behind him.

"Don't be a wuss," Gary Parnell whispered back to the complainer.

"Lay off him, Gary," Derek said.

Sam shot Derek a silent *Thank you* with his eyes.

Sam Rockman was always scuffling to get a passing grade. He was very nice, but some things took him a little longer to understand—like math. And science.

Gary Parnell, on the other hand, was the class brainiac—which would have been fine, except that he loved to brag about it. Especially to Derek, whom Gary considered his biggest rival.

Gary insisted on making every quiz and every test a contest between the two of them—just to prove who was smarter.

Derek never backed away from the challenge—which was probably why Gary never got tired of beating him. Derek could count on one hand the number of times he'd come out ahead, but that didn't stop him from trying even harder the next time.

On the other hand, when it came to anything involving sports or exercise, Gary usually got a D at best—if not an

F. He always acted like it was torture to break a sweat. Last spring, when he'd been forced to play baseball by his mom and wound up on Derek's team, he'd spent the first three weeks of the season complaining nonstop.

Ms. Terrapin cleared her throat, a signal for the class to quiet down. "Before we move on to sixth-grade work, though, we're going to test what you've already learned. Or at least how much of it you've retained over the summer."

She started passing out test booklets. The kids in front handed them back until they reached the rear of the classroom. Derek noticed that Sam took his reluctantly, with a little shudder of dread.

"As you may know, national standardized tests are coming next spring. They're very different from what you've experienced—and they test everything you've ever learned. So naturally they take a lot of time to prepare for." Another murmur went through the class; a soft ripple of worry.

"So we are giving you a 'pretest.' In addition to giving you valuable practice, it will help us measure your current levels of learning. Don't worry—your scores won't count this time around. But for those of you who are behind and need more help, we'll be recommending after-school study and tutoring between now and next spring."

"Yikes!" said Sam, fidgeting nervously in his seat. "*Extra* study? Tutoring?"

Gary pretended to yawn. "It's good to be a genius," he whispered to Derek. "I get to spend all *my* extra time playing computer games."

"The practice exams will be on September twentieth and twenty-first," said Ms. Terrapin. "One day for English and one day for math. We will be using last year's tests to practice on. Between now and then we will be reviewing for it. I will expect you to go through these study booklets at home."

She stood behind her desk, a gleam in her eye. "Now. Principal Parker has offered a *special pizza party* to the class that does the best. As the world's biggest pizza fan, I expect my class to bring home the pie!"

That got a big cheer—although there were plenty of nervous looks going around too.

"Je-Ter . . . pre-pare to be de-feat-ed!" Gary said, using his best sci-fi robot voice.

"Who's that supposed to sound like?" Derek shot back. "Frankenstein?"

"Don't you know anything? It's *Jar-El*, the final boss!"

"Huh?"

"From *DoomMaster*," Gary explained, as if Derek were a two-year-old and didn't know his fingers from his toes.

"Oooh. Okay," Derek said doubtfully. "Gotta say, I've never heard of *Jar-El*—or *DoomMaster*. Just so you know, though—I am *not* going to be de-feat-ed on this test. Not by Jar-El, and definitely not by you, *Par-Nell*."

Smack-talking was one thing, but actually beating

Gary out on a test that measured *everything they'd ever learned*? That was going to take a lot of extra studying between now and the twentieth!

"Here's something else to take home," said Ms. Terrapin, handing back another bunch of papers. "Applications for the Fall Talent Show."

"Yesss!" Vijay Patel said, pumping his fist. He looked across the room to Derek, waving the form at him excitedly and pointing at it with his other hand.

Derek had completely forgotten about the Fall Talent Show. Now he remembered that he and Vijay had talked about it over the summer—or *written* about it, to be more accurate.

Vijay had been halfway around the world in India last summer, attending a family wedding with his mom and dad—which was why he hadn't joined Derek and Dave at the lake.

Vijay had written though—all about his gigantic family and Indian wedding customs. He'd also suggested the two of them work up a break dance routine for the Fall Talent Show.

Derek had sort of said "okay" . . . then proceeded to forget all about it. But obviously Vijay had *not* forgotten. Not at all.

"All right, class, you can start packing up your things," said the teacher. "The bell's about to—and there it goes," she finished as the bell chimed in right on cue.

"Better start cramming, Jeter," Gary said. "Oh no! Is

that *sweat* on your forehead? You wouldn't be *worried*, now, would you?"

"Not a chance," Derek shot back, showing more confidence than he felt. "Forget *Jar-El*—I am *Je-Ter,* and *you* are going to find out who's the *real* final boss."

"Wait up, Derek!"

Vijay came up to him as he was repacking his book bag in the hallway.

"Hi, Vij."

"So cool, right? You and me in the talent show?" He put out his hand for a high five.

"Definitely," Derek said.

Truth was, the idea of the two of them break-dancing onstage *did* seem like fun. It definitely would make everyone at school stand up and take notice. He and Vijay sometimes fooled around with dance moves when they were over at each other's houses—but nobody at school knew either of them were into it.

If Derek wasn't all that enthusiastic right at the moment, it was because his mind was focused on outscoring Gary on the big test. Creating a talent show act definitely was going to infringe on his study and review time.

"So, let's get going!" Vijay said happily. His parents both worked late at the hospital on Thursdays and wouldn't be home till six, so the two boys had planned to spend the afternoon together at Derek's.

"Last one on the bus is a rotten egg!" Derek said—and the race was on.

Derek got to the school's front lobby way ahead of Vijay. And there was Dave, staring at something posted on the big bulletin board.

"Derek! Check this out!"

Derek looked over his shoulder for Vijay but couldn't see him through the crowd of kids cramming the lobby, all of them trying to get out the door at once.

"What is it?"

"AAU basketball tryouts at the Y!"

"Whoa! Already?"

"A week from Saturday! Are you psyched?"

"Totally!"

"We're gonna have to get our game in gear," Dave said.

Just then a breathless Vijay finally made his way over to them. "I couldn't get through that mob!" he said, laughing. "You are way too fast for me, Derek."

"Hi, Vij," said Dave.

"Hi, Dave. Hey, Derek, we'd better get going. The bus is going to leave without us!"

"Talk to you later, Derek," said Dave, who always got driven home and never took the bus. "We've got to make some plans."

"Definitely!" Derek waved, then followed Vijay out to the bus, his head spinning. Fifteen minutes ago he'd been looking at an easy, relaxed weekend. Now he was looking at a three-ring circus!

Chapter Two

The two boys sat at Derek's kitchen table, going over their review booklets. Derek's mom was working till six at her accounting job. Although his dad taught classes at the university in the mornings each weekday as well as three evenings a week, he was usually home by now.

But at the moment he was still out with Sharlee at her dance class—or was it karate today? Derek couldn't remember—his little sister was even busier than he was. Obviously, though, that was about to change.

"I think we should look over your music collection," Vijay was saying now. "I haven't got that many good CDs."

"Come on, man, we've got to keep studying," Derek said. "There's a ton of stuff here to review before the twentieth."

"Yes, but we are going to do fine, Derek! We are the best test-takers in the whole class, except for—"

"—for Gary Parnell," Derek finished the sentence. "I know, I know. That's just it."

"I don't get it," said Vijay with a puzzled look.

Derek started to speak, then stopped himself. "Never mind. It's too dumb to even waste time talking about. But I do think we need to keep going over this stuff. I want to make sure we know everything in this booklet backward and forward."

"Okay," said Vijay, backing off. "But maybe we can at least check out some music after? I mean, we *can't* just go up onstage and expect to do a break dance number! We have to plan it all out first and then put in *lots* of time practicing. You know what they say? They say, 'Practice makes perfect!'"

"Well, we'll still have a week after the test . . ."

"Derek, you know all those other kids will be doing stuff they've done for years. We are probably the only ones making up our act from scratch!"

"I know. But—"

"Look, don't worry," Vijay said. "We are both super-good dancers. We just have to figure out what we're going to *do*—and then, of course, practice doing it over and over and over again. If we do that, we are sure to win the contest!"

"Mmm," said Derek. "No pressure, right?"

Vijay laughed. "You are very funny. So what do you say

about this weekend? We can figure out our routine, pick out our music . . ."

"Uh . . . sure," Derek said, eager to change the subject. "But right now we need to get back to work."

Being in the talent show was all well and good, but not if it meant having to listen to Gary's mocking *Jar-El* voice for the rest of the semester!

"We were on page twenty-three, at the top. One fourth of one fourth equals . . ."

The phone rang. Derek got up from the kitchen table to answer it.

"Hello?"

"Hey, it's me!"

"Hey, Dave, what's up?"

"When are you free to get together and practice, man? We can use the court at my house this weekend. What do you say?"

Dave lived in a big house with a pool, a golf hole—and, best of all, a tricked-out sports court. And his family had their own personal driver, named Chase, who also served as Dave's guardian whenever his parents were away on business—which was a lot.

"Sure thing! I'll talk to my parents." Derek looked over at Vijay, who was waiting expectantly for him to get off the phone—and he suddenly realized he had a problem. "Uh, listen, Dave, I'm kind of busy right now. Can we talk about it tomorrow?"

He didn't mention to Dave that Vijay was in the room with him. Nor did he say anything that would clue Vijay in to what he and Dave were talking about.

Vijay and Dave were his two best friends—but sometimes it was hard not to make one of them feel like Derek was favoring the other.

"Oh, okay," said Dave. "Talk to you later, then!"

"What was that all about?" Vijay asked after Derek hung up. "He sounded pretty excited."

Derek gave a casual shrug. "Basketball tryouts over at the Y."

"Oh. Yeah, that *is* pretty cool." Vijay smiled, but they both knew that basketball wasn't his sport.

"You . . . you want to try out with us?"

"No, not me. I like baseball and soccer. But basketball? I never understand the dribbling, with only so many steps in between bounces. And the net is too tiny and too far away for my liking!"

Derek laughed. Vijay was always cracking him up.

"Anyway, that's next Saturday, not this one," Vijay went on. "Lucky for us. We'd better put in some time on our act this weekend, don't you think?"

"Yeah. . . ."

Until the moment Ms. Terrapin had handed out their test booklets, Derek's plan for the weekend had been to watch the big Yankees-Tigers series on TV on Saturday, then spend Sunday with his family as usual.

But now, suddenly, everything had been thrown into chaos. He had agreed to meet with two different friends, to practice two different things. And on top of it all, he had to review *everything he'd ever learned* in school—all on Saturday!

It was Mission: Impossible*!*

"So?" Vijay asked.

"Well, it can't be on Sunday . . . that's always family day around here."

"Saturday, then!" Vijay said, smiling. "That's fine. When do you think—morning or afternoon?"

"Um, I'll let you know tomorrow."

"Cool. Let's do our talent show applications before I go."

Just as they finished filling out their forms, the front door opened, and Mr. Jeter came in, followed by Sharlee.

"Hey, you two!" Mr. Jeter greeted them. "What are you up to?"

"Reviewing for a big test," Vijay replied. "And planning our act for the Fall Talent Show!"

"*Talent*?" Mr. Jeter repeated with a twinkle in his eyes. "And which of your many, many talents would that be?"

Derek and Vijay laughed. "Don't tell him—not yet," Derek told Vijay. "It'll be a surprise for you, Dad."

"Tell *me*! Tell *me*!" Sharlee begged, jumping up and down, making her frilly dance skirt bounce along with her.

"No way—you'll just blab to everyone," Derek said, laughing.

"*I will not!* My lips are sealed! See?" She pretended to lock her lips with an invisible key. "Mmm . . . mmmm . . . mmm!"

"Okay, okay, I'll tell you—*later*," Derek conceded. *"Maybe."*

"I'd better get home," Vijay said, gathering up his school stuff. "My parents will be wondering what's keeping me. See you tomorrow, Derek! Don't forget to bring the application with you tomorrow. Bye, all!"

Derek, Sharlee, and Mr. Jeter got to work getting dinner ready. By the time Mrs. Jeter came home, the table was set, the salad made, the vegetables all cut up, and the chicken warming in the oven. All she had to do was drop her briefcase, sit down, and eat!

After dinner Derek helped her dry the dishes. Only when they were done, and the whole family had settled down in the living room, did he bring up his thorny scheduling problem.

"Dad? Mom? Could I go over to Dave's on Saturday afternoon? We need to practice for the under-twelve basketball tryouts."

"Didn't you say you have a lot of reviewing to do?" his mom asked.

"Yes, but it's stuff we've *already learned*. And the test isn't until the twentieth."

"Sometimes we forget a lot over the summer," Derek's dad pointed out. "You told us there's a ton of material to go over. So you need make sure you put aside enough time for it."

"I'm *going* to—a *lot*! But basketball tryouts are next Saturday! Dave and I both want to be on the team, so we need to practice every minute we can between now and then. I can study after that!"

"You're talking about the league down at the Y?" his mom asked.

"Uh-huh. Only the best players make it, Mom! I know Dave and I can do it, though—*if we're prepared enough*. He's got this great sports court at his house. . . ."

Mr. and Mrs. Jeter exchanged glances. "Wouldn't it save you time if Dave came here?" his mom asked.

"Mom, the courts here are all messed up! The rims are bent, and the pavement's cracked. Dave's court is *really awesome*!"

"Wait, now," said his dad. "Didn't you and Vijay say you were preparing something for the talent show? Didn't I hear you tell him you were going to get together on Saturday?"

"There's also the Yankees-Tigers game," Derek added.

"It sounds like you've gotten yourself overcommitted, at least for this weekend," said Mrs. Jeter.

"You said you'd tell me what you were going to do in the show!" Sharlee reminded Derek. "Tell me now! Tell me!"

"We're not even exactly sure yet," Derek confessed to her. "That's why we need to get together," he told his parents. "To figure out what we're going to do."

"It's an awful lot, son," said his dad. "Are you totally sure you want to commit yourself to so many projects? It's hard to do a lot of things well when you're doing them all at once."

"I *am* committed!" Derek insisted. "I mean . . . I'm *pretty sure* I am. . . ."

"So when do you plan to fit all this in?" asked his mom.

"Um . . . that's where I was hoping you could give me some advice," he said.

"Derek," said his dad, "I think you're going to have to eliminate something—at least for this weekend. And it's not going to be our Sunday afternoon, either. We've got a picnic planned, over at the university."

Derek realized there was only one thing he could sacrifice and still keep his commitments. "I guess I won't get to watch the game," he said softly, looking down at the carpet.